the Dublin Review

number seventy-eight | SPRING 2020

EDITOR & PUBLISHER: BRENDAN BARRINGTON
DEPUTY PUBLISHERS: DEANNA ORTIZ & AINGEALA FLANNERY

The Dublin Review, number seventy-eight (Spring 2020).
Design by Atelier David Smith. Printed by Naas Printing Ltd.

ISBN 978-1-9161337-2-3

SUBMISSIONS: Please go to www.thedublinreview.com and follow the instructions on the 'Submissions' page. Although we encourage electronic submissions, we also accept physical submissions, to The Dublin Review, P.O. Box 7948, Dublin 1, Ireland. We cannot return physical manuscripts, so please do not send a unique or irreplaceable piece of work, and be sure to include your email address for a reply. *The Dublin Review* assumes no responsibility for unsolicited material.

SUBSCRIPTIONS: *The Dublin Review* is published quarterly. A subscription costs €34 / UK£26 per year in Ireland & Northern Ireland, €45 / UK£36 / US$60 per year for the rest of the world. Institutions add €15 / UK£13 / US$20. To subscribe or to order back issues, please use the secure-ordering facility at www.thedublinreview.com. Alternatively, you may send your address and a cheque or Visa/MC data and order details to Subscriptions, The Dublin Review, P.O. Box 7948, Dublin 1, Ireland. Credit-card orders are billed at the euro price. Please indicate if credit-card billing address differs from mailing address. If you have a question regarding an order, please email us at order@thedublinreview.com.

WEBSITE: www.thedublinreview.com

TRADE SALES: *The Dublin Review* is distributed to the trade by Gill & Macmillan Distribution, Hume Avenue, Park West, Dublin 12.

SALES REPRESENTATION: Robert Towers, 2 The Crescent, Monkstown, Co. Dublin, tel +353 1 2806532, fax +353 1 2806020.

The Dublin Review receives financial assistance from the Arts Council.

Contents | *number seventy-eight* | SPRING 2020

Sunshine state

EOIN BUTLER

July 2018

1

The flight into Orlando was uneventful. I don't recall what meal option I chose, or what movie I sat through. I do recall a group of passengers in floral shirts ordering endless rounds of drinks from the trolley cart. I regarded them with the sort of mild trepidation with which, in happier times, my fellow long-haul passengers might once have regarded me. I pulled the cowboy hat I was wearing down over my eyes and tried to get some rest.

Guidebooks warn travellers not to visit Florida in the months of July or August. But I hadn't read any guidebooks. In fact, I hadn't done much of anything in a while. My mental health had taken a serious knock the previous autumn and hadn't really recovered. I'm not going to talk about what happened. Suffice to say it was an experience that left me feeling anxious, vulnerable and extremely paranoid.

I was, in any case, a veteran of road trips in the American South. Every year, my young niece travelled from Dublin to Savannah, Georgia, where she spent time with her father. This time, my sister had accompanied Lola on the outward leg of her journey; my job was to bring the child home. With ten free days at my disposal before that, my half-formed plan was to visit the most southerly point in the continental United States: Key West, a beach community closer as the crow flies to Havana than it is to Miami. Who knew? Maybe a week of hammocks, beach balls and margaritas would pull me out of the black hole into which I felt myself slipping.

At the car rental desk, a long tailback of holidaymakers were either sitting on their suitcases or sprawled out scowling on the floor. The franchise had run out of cars. Most of the staff were hiding out in the break room, leaving one junior employee alone to man the desk. In the clammy heat of a packed airport concourse, I removed the black cowboy hat from my head and set it down on the carpet. It was a souvenir I'd picked up in New Mexico a year earlier. I never saw it again.

Eventually, I was handed the keys of a white Ford Focus. I steered the vehicle out of the parking garage and into the blinding light of midday.

Central Florida was terror in technicolour. I sensed panthers' eyes blinking in the palm trees as I tore along an insane eight-lane highway, with testy truckers and pick-up drivers zipping past my wing mirrors at close quarters on either side. My destination that day was St Petersburg, about a hundred miles west, on the far side of Tampa Bay. Partly, I wanted to visit the city's Salvador Dalí museum. Mostly, I just wanted to put some distance between myself and the theme-park hordes.

The car's onboard GPS wasn't working. But St Petersburg is one of the largest cities in the state. It was bound to be well signposted. I figured I'd sit tight in the slow lane, on the right, and wait for my exit to appear. But when the exit for St Petersburg did materialize, the sign directed me to a ramp splitting off to the left, which gave me about five hundred metres in which to cut across four packed lanes of high-speed, high-strung traffic. At one point, when no clear opportunity to change lane presented itself, I simply hit the indicator, paused a beat, then swerved hard left. The enormous eighteen-wheeler closing in hard behind me, honking its horn, appeared in my rear-view mirror like a whale gliding in to swallow a piece of plankton.

Having missed the exit, I managed to type 'saint petersburg' into Google Maps on my phone. But several times in the endless spaghetti junctions, the phone's screen locked, and I had to re-type the PIN code with clammy fingers, while simultaneously keeping the car between the lines at 80 m.p.h. At one point, an elderly African-American motorcyclist, dressed like a cross between a matador and a Hell's Angel, whom I'd presumably cut off while changing lanes, pulled up alongside my window waving his fist and yelling abuse at me. I pretended not to notice him. When, finally, I came to a stop in a Walmart parking lot in Pinellas Park, on the outskirts of St Petersburg, I sat shaking in the driver's seat for a couple of minutes before alighting from the car.

2

That afternoon, I went for a stroll on the boardwalk at St Pete Beach. A group of grey-haired retirees were sitting under palm trees playing bridge, canasta and shuffleboard. On the other side of the walkway, a lone pelican was hunched over a mooring post. Below him, bone-white sands stretched down to meet the Gulf of Mexico. I wandered into a little beach shack called Felix's Aquarium. The owner was a laid-back local, dressed in a khaki vest, shorts and flip-flops. He told me he made a good living selling tropical fish to tourists. Business was slow that day, however, and he seemed happy to chat.

This was the off season, he said. Lots of the retirees who winter in St Petersburg head back north in summer to avoid the heat. He made us both espressos. Then he gave me a tour of the shop. He showed me Torpedo Skates, Guitar Fish, Horse-Killer Eels, Mud Fish and West Indian Scorpionfish. He plucked one fearsome-looking customer, whose name I didn't catch, out of its tank and thrust it toward me in jest. I told him I'd encountered characters far scarier on the Florida highway system that morning. Felix laughed. He listened to my laundry list of complaints about Florida traffic with good humour and conceded that getting to grips with those vast frenetic highways can take time for an outsider. But he assured me I'd get used to it.

What about the insane speeds people drive? 'Well, I'll grant you that,' he said. I told him that, at first, I assumed I could slow down and drive at my own pace. But any time I slowed down, and allowed even a sliver of a gap to open up between myself and the vehicle in front of me, some maniac with a death wish would weave right in between us. And, if I didn't immediately speed up again, another maniac would weave in behind him. And another.

And if the internet was to be believed, I added, at least one of them was likely to be a meth addict with an alligator in the trunk.

Felix took a sip from his espresso. He wasn't smiling anymore.

That was a Florida Man joke, I said.

'I get that,' he replied.

Florida Man was a hugely popular Twitter account that recycled, for comedic purposes, colourful headlines from the state's local press in which the words 'Florida man' had been used as shorthand for any member of the public who had fallen foul of the law. The account's greatest hits included 'Florida man tries to pick up prostitute while driving school bus', 'Florida man arrested for murder after pocket-dialling 911' and 'Florida man charged with assault after throwing alligator through Wendy's drive-thru window'. For fans of the account, the humour lay in pretending that these were not random, unrelated local crimes, but rather the work of a single individual.

By that summer of 2018, however, the joke didn't seem quite so funny anymore. Commentators didn't have to dig deep to discover that the true stories behind these lurid headlines were mostly sad human tales of addiction, mental illness and – surprisingly often – alligator abuse. What bothered Felix wasn't just that these jokes tended to punch down. He resented the damage he saw them doing to Florida's image around the world. 'Ten years ago,' he said, 'when you thought of Florida, what did you think of?' Space shuttles, theme parks and sandy beaches, I answered. 'Whereas nowadays?' Shirtless sex offenders with face tattoos. 'Exactly,' he said.

What was worse, he claimed, was that this perception wasn't even well deserved. Under Florida's unique Sunshine Law, police incident reports were made available to the public without restriction, which completely skewed the way the state is portrayed in the press. He seemed to be suggesting that people shouldn't take everything they read on the internet at face value.

Well, that was a thought.

3

Okay, none of that last section is true. I didn't take a stroll down St Pete Beach. I didn't meet a man named Felix who showed me some exotic fish and helpfully got me up to speed on cultural discourse surrounding the Florida Man meme. I actually just read a bunch of online articles cited on the Florida Man Wikipedia page, while lying on my bed at the Tampa Bay Red Roof Inn. As I was reading, I could hear three inebriated men on the footpath directly outside my window conspiring in low voices. Initially, I was concerned they might be planning to steal my car, which was parked directly outside. Only later, it occurred to me the greater danger would be if they broke through the flimsy wooden door separating us and entered my motel room.

I listened to them plotting for hours. Then I fell asleep.

4

Sometimes, the best thing about flying blind on holiday is not feeling obliged to see all the must-see local attractions. Other times, it's stumbling upon them quite by accident. I left St Petersburg next morning intent only on getting the hell out of central Florida. On previous trips, I'd felt most at home among the green fields, blue skies and open roads of Tennessee and the Carolinas. Poring over Google Maps, I decided that the vast wilderness of the Everglades in southern Florida might offer a similar experience.

I got on I-275, heading south out of the city – and then suddenly found myself skimming like a stone across the clear blue water of Tampa Bay. The Sunshine Skyway Bridge is a spectacular five-mile-long, cable-stayed structure not dissimilar to the Pont de Saint-Nazaire over the river Loire in France, which my father had driven us across on a family holiday once when I was a child. One moment, I was riding so low over the water I could practically reach out the driver's-side window and scoop fish from the water. The next, I was a hundred metres up in the air, eyeballing a helicopter pilot and his passengers, who were enjoying an aerial tour of the bay.

Over breakfast at a roadside diner in Manatee County, two older couples – one white, the other African-American – were chatting to an African-American waitress about an incident that occurred a few days earlier, in the nearby city of Clearwater. Apparently, an old man had gotten into a dispute with a young man over a disabled parking space. When the young man refused to back down, the old man produced a gun and fired a shot at him. 'Just goes to show,' the white husband said, ruefully. 'When you pick a fight with a stranger, you never know who you're going up against.' The others nodded their heads in apparent agreement.

I couldn't help but smile. The previous evening, I'd let some (possibly rogue) Wikipedia editor convince me that Florida Man jokes were a baseless slander against a blameless state. Hours later, this doozy of a riposte to that argument had just landed in my lap. Florida pensioner shoots motorist in argument over disabled parking space? The tweet wrote itself.

I pulled out my phone to learn a little more about this story. Unfortunately, the unabridged version proved considerably less hilarious than the imagined Florida Man headline. It seemed this racially mixed group of elderly strangers, whom I'd overheard making polite chit-chat across the counter at a roadside diner, had got some of their facts wrong, and hadn't seen fit to mention some pretty key details about the shooting. The shooter was not an old man; he was only 47, a white guy called Michael Drejka. Also, he hadn't just taken a shot at the younger man. He'd killed him.

His victim was an African-American man named Markeis McGlockton. As per the *Tampa Bay Times*:

> At about 3:30 p.m., Markeis McGlockton stopped by the Circle A Food Store at 1201 Sunset Point Road near Clearwater. His girlfriend, Britany Jacobs, parked in a handicap-reserved spot outside the convenience store and waited in the car with two of the couple's children — 4 months and 3 at the time. McGlockton, 28, went into the store with their third child, Markeis Jr., who was 5.
>
> Michael Drejka, 47, pulled into the parking lot and approached Jacobs, who was 25. He asked Jacobs why she had parked in the spot if she didn't have a handicap-designated plate or placard. The two started arguing. It escalated to the point that others in the parking lot started paying attention.
>
> One of the witnesses entered the store and reported what was going on. McGlockton stepped back outside, walked up to Drejka and shoved him to the ground. Drejka pulled out a .40-caliber Glock handgun and shot McGlockton once in the chest. McGlockton was taken to Morton Plant Hospital and pronounced dead shortly after. The entire incident was caught on the store's surveillance video.

Since the shooting, other motorists had come forward with stories of similar run-ins they'd had with Drejka. In one case, Drejka was alleged to have racially abused and threatened to shoot an African-American truck driver outside the very same convenience store. The store owner described Drejka as basically a crank who routinely picked fights with people over parking spaces and said he'd had to call the cops on him before.

I pulled the CCTV footage up on my phone. In the video, McGlockton emerges from the convenience store, sees Drejka aggressively confronting his partner, and pushes Drejka to the ground. Drejka gets up onto his knees and aims a gun at McGlockton, who then turns around and appears about to walk away when Drejka fires the fatal shot. It was, on the face of it, about as open-and-shut a homicide case as you could imagine – but the local county sheriff didn't arrest Drejka at the scene, citing Florida's notorious 'Stand Your Ground' law. At that time, he was widely expected never to face justice. (Eventually, Drejka was charged, tried, convicted of manslaughter and sentenced to twenty years in prison.)

I paid for breakfast and hit I-75 south. The highway was empty. About 150 miles south of St Petersburg, near the city of Naples, the road veered sharply to the left. I was now entering the Everglades. Dark clouds were gathering overhead, but I put the hammer down and blundered on into the swamp.

4

It was shortly before lunchtime when I pulled up at the Collier County Rest Area on the Everglades Parkway, also known as Alligator Alley. The sun was peeking out from behind the clouds and the foliage was humming with the sound of a thousand exotic insects. The humidity was intense. But it appeared I might, for now, have just outrun the storm.

I got out of the car to stretch my legs. An old soldier was sitting by a table in the shade. The fatigues he was wearing had seen better days. The Marine and Army-branded T-shirts and baseball caps he was selling were clearly knock-offs. The woman ahead of me, who handed him a couple of bucks, didn't ask for anything in return. The only thing about this guy that looked legit was his military I.D., which was prominently displayed. This was something I'd noticed in the United States. Panhandling is permissible. Bootlegging is tolerated. But posing as a military veteran, if you haven't earned those stripes, is strictly prohibited under a federal law called the Stolen Valor Act.

The taboo against 'stolen valor' isn't just enforced by law. A YouTube search reveals thousands of videos of impostor soldiers being called out by vigilante members of the public. In the videos, the impostors rarely come across like master criminals. They are usually harmless attention-seekers whose worst crime was accepting a cup of coffee from a stranger under false pretences. Their tormentors, by contrast, often appear aggressive and self-righteous. In many cases, these vigilantes seem like bullies.

I was indoors now, pissing into a bizarrely oversized porcelain urinal. In my determination to remain hydrated, I'd consumed three one-litre bottles of mineral water in the car that morning, and the process of voiding my bladder was taking a little longer than usual. Eventually, the motion-activated over-head light went out. I was shooting in the dark. I froze. The urinal was the world's largest bullseye and I was firing at it from point-blank range. But I couldn't take the shot. I was afraid that my aim might be off. I was afraid that some of that piss I'd been bursting to let go of might spray back and hit me.

In the car park outside, an enormous black bird was standing on the tar-mac directly in my path. At first I thought it might be a turkey. But when a couple more of his mates swooped down from the sky to join him, I had to revise that opinion. Soon a dozen of these malevolent-looking creatures were standing between me and my parked car. I went back to the soldier at the table in the shade and asked him what they were. 'Turkey vultures,' he said. Are they dangerous, I asked? He shrugged. 'They'll slash tyres and pull out windshield wipers,' he said. 'But they don't usually attack humans. Not adults, anyway.'

I strolled back to grab another large bottle of mineral water from the vending machine. Those vultures could move on at their own leisure. I wasn't going to disturb them.

5

There had been no gas pumps at the Collier County Rest Area, or anywhere else along Alligator Alley, and the fuel gauge was flatlining by the time I chanced upon the Miccosukee Service Plaza, still in the middle of nowhere. There wasn't much traffic on the highway, but there were at least two or three vehicles backed up at each of the twenty or so fuel pumps. When my turn came, I stepped out of the car. The sky overhead was dark and cloudy, but the air was hot. Rainwater about two inches deep was covering the entire forecourt, but I hadn't witnessed a single drop falling. An eerie calm prevailed as I pumped the gas. The German national flags that for some reason festooned the place were barely fluttering. (These, I later learned, were the colours of the Seminole nation.)

After filling the tank, I headed inside to pay. Stepping through that muddy rainwater in sandals felt like sloshing around in a warm bath. The shop had a deli advertised, but it was only selling corn dogs and other fast food. Down the back there were stuffed alligator toys on a shelf. I considered buying one for my nephew at home. But I tugged a little at the stitching and decided it wasn't worth the price they were charging. I paid for my fuel, got back in the car and pressed on.

I turned on the car stereo. Conservative talk radio was ablaze with discussion of the Clearwater shooting. Callers were seething. It was an outrage. It was unacceptable. It was symptomatic of a deep-rooted societal problem that needed to be addressed. The host fielded call after call from angry listeners unanimous in their denunciation of Britney Jacobs for having parked briefly in a handicapped parking space. And if you think I'm joking about that, then you haven't spent much time listening to American conservative talk radio.

The host did briefly acknowledge reports that Michael Drejka had a history of racially abusing African-American motorists. He admitted that, if true, this would put quite a different complexion on the case. But that point immediately died on the vine.

When a representative of the Clearwater police department called in, the host demanded to know why officers arriving on the scene hadn't issued Britney Jacobs with a ticket for illegal parking. The police representative replied that since Jacobs' children had just witnessed their father being shot dead, issuing their mother with a $25 city ordinance fine might have been deemed insensitive in the circumstances. The host seemed genuinely stumped by this response. He paused a moment to consider it. Then he conceded the cop might have a point and moved on.

One caller was a bit uncomfortable with concealed-carry gun permits. He was an old-timer who told the host, 'In my day, those two gentlemen would have had a fistfight, then shaken hands and wished each other a good day.' The show then cut to an advert for erectile-dysfunction pills.

6

Further down the highway, a succession of electronic roadside signs advised motorists to 'Move Over For Stopped Emergency Vehicles'. The previous summer, I'd driven a thousand miles across Texas and noticed similar signs warning motorists not to leave small children or pets in parked cars. Those Texan warnings made sense at least, even if the frequency with which they were offered seemed like overkill.

Driving in Alabama and Mississippi, the summer before that, signs had warned 'Bridge Ices Before Road'. I was at least two days chewing over those four words before I worked out what they meant in that particular order. But 'Move Over For Stopped Emergency Vehicles' was a conundrum on a whole other level. Did Floridians really require regular reminders not to ram their cars into parked ambulances? On the evidence of what I'd seen so far … the jury was out.

I wasn't far from Miami now. With about six million inhabitants, Miami is technically Florida's most populous metropolis. Culturally, however, the self-proclaimed Capital of Latin America is in a whole other hemisphere. I had planned to find a hostel or a motel somewhere in the Everglades. But now I decided to make a break for the border. *Vamos a Miami* ...

Then the skies opened. By the time Alligator Alley collided with the Sawgrass Expressway, it was like all the spaghetti junctions of Central Florida had reunited for one insane gala encore performance in the rain. The golf-ball-sized knot of stress in the back of my neck, which had been in abeyance since I crossed the Sunshine Skyway Bridge that morning, was now back to bursting point.

I'd seen monsoon rain before, in Asia and Africa. But never from the wheel of a speeding car on a crowded twelve-lane highway. The rain wasn't just pouring down. It was bouncing back up off the ground. It was being spat backwards by the tyres of vehicles in front and sprayed sideways across my windscreen by vehicles passing on either side. For once in Florida, I was glad to be driving a hatchback. The larger trucks and lorries in front were visibly swaying in the wind. Beyond them, I could make out palm trees thrashing from side to side.

I got off the Expressway, thinking that might improve things. It wound up making them a thousand times worse. The Expressway was up on stilts. It drained easily. Heading through Westview on Florida 924, water was gathering in enormous pools on both sides of the road. It was still six-lane traffic, but now there were lights and crosswalks to negotiate. Conditions were rapidly deteriorating. I felt like I was in one of those old black-and-white B-movies where the protagonist is driving but there's no budget for scenery, so the director just has stagehands pour enormous vats of water down the front of the windscreen to simulate heavy rain.

There were about six inches of floodwater on the road. In the blink of an eye, that became a foot. Odds were that driver of the pick-up truck in front of me was a native Floridian. Even if he wasn't, he had to know better how to cope with these conditions than I did, since I had no idea. Therefore, I would copy whatever he did. If he drove forward, I'd drive forward. If he stopped, I'd stop. And if he abandoned his vehicle, I'd do the same.

It didn't take long to identify the flaw in this plan. The pick-up I was following was a couple of feet higher off the ground than my hatchback. What was safe for him wasn't necessarily safe for me. Heading into the next intersection, the road took a dip and, based on the water levels against his tyres, it appeared as though the surge was now closer to eighteen inches in depth. The pick-up in front of me plunged forward into the flood. I looked around wondering what to do next. Simultaneously, there was a blinding flash of light, a low rumble and a very distinct thump on the roof of my car.

My car had just been struck by lightning.

7

The car was now stopped dead at an intersection in north Miami. I patted myself down. Incredibly, I seemed to be okay.

Most of the other drivers had stopped too. It was time to make a decision. I peered out the driver's-side window. Frankly, I wouldn't have been surprised to see a cow float by on a cabin roof. I could just make out a bowling alley about a hundred metres away. The rucksack containing all of my possessions was lying on the back seat. I figured I could grab the bag, open the driver's-side door and wade to the sanctuary of the bowling alley. But I didn't want to be too hasty. I had no idea what the financial repercussions of abandoning a hire car at a busy urban intersection might be. I took a deep breath and counted to thirty. Then it stopped raining.

Ten minutes later, I was driving on the Julia Tuttle Causeway across Biscayne Bay. The sky was blue and the road was bone dry. It was as though the storm had never happened.

That evening I took a room at Red, a boutique hotel on Miami Beach. After dropping off my bag, I wandered down to a small Cuban restaurant in the Art Deco district and asked for a table. The waitress handed me a menu, showing pictures of about a dozen traditional Cuban dishes. I pointed at the menu and asked if there was any particular dish she'd recommend. She exhaled loudly and went back into the kitchen to find someone who could speak English.

Already, I was wondering if anyone at home would believe the story of the day I'd just had. While I waited for my food order to arrive, I scrolled backwards through my phone's camera roll. I had photos of the black turkey vultures surrounding my car and of the petrol station forecourt under water. I had video of myself driving through monsoon rain on a heavily flooded road in the outskirts of Miami. (Foolhardy on my part, I suppose. I was like one of those tourists on a balcony who takes a video of the incoming tsunami, not realising their hotel is going to be smithereens in about seven seconds.) What I didn't have was anything to support my contention that my car had been hit by lightning.

I contacted my cousin in New Mexico. He isn't a mechanic or a meteorologist. But he lives in Las Cruces, which qualifies him as an expert on electrical storms in my book. I told him I'd been in monsoon rain in busy traffic, on a road covered with at least a foot of floodwater, when the incident occurred. Every time a vehicle overtook me on either side, a large volume of water would hit the side of my car, cascading in a rolling wave from back to front. The lightning bolt that hit me made a distinctly different sound. This was a single, unmistakable thump, equivalent to a plastic football bouncing off the roof of the car. It happened at precisely the same moment I heard a roar of thunder and saw a blinding flash of light. And nothing, subsequently, had fallen down off the roof. On that basis, I had concluded that my car had been hit by lightning.

My cousin was sceptical. He asked whether the car's electronics were affected. I said they weren't. They continued to work as before. He also asked me if there was any visible damage to the roof of the car. There wasn't. 'If you don't have any burn marks or functional problems with the car,' he said, 'then you probably didn't get hit directly. It probably hit next to you or somewhere close by.'

8

I couldn't sleep much that night. When I did sleep, I had bad dreams. In the most vivid of these, I was at the airport in Savannah with my niece. I'd lost her passport and we couldn't board our flight. Her grandparents and Homeland Security were all pretty pissed off with me. But Lola had faith. She kept looking up at me with hope in her eyes, like she knew I was going to produce the passport at the last moment and prove the naysayers wrong. But I didn't. The passport was gone. I couldn't account for it.

I woke up yet again with a start. It was a few minutes shy of 7 a.m. I wasn't getting back to sleep now. I got up, dressed myself and threw a hotel bath towel into a plastic bag to sneak it past reception. I took the elevator down to the lobby and wandered across the road to the beach. It was a Wednesday morning: a working day for locals. The tourists, also, must have all been sleeping off hangovers from the night before, because Miami Beach, one of the most famous beaches in the world, was completely deserted. There literally wasn't another human as far as I could see in either direction.

I undressed, arranged my clothes into a neat little pile and plunged into the ocean. I swam fifty or sixty metres out to sea, then I turned back towards the shore and sloshed around. It was an unforgettable sight. The beach was lined with palm trees and, behind them, I could see the tops of all of these beautiful old-fashioned hotel fronts. I turned over on my back and wiggled my toes in the air. This, I told myself, is what Key West will be like. All of the stress and the self-doubt that had been crippling me for months would finally dissolve in that warm ocean water. Even still, I kept a sharp eye back toward that neat little pile of my clothes on the beach to make sure no one made off with them.

After spending the better part of an hour in the water, I headed back to the hotel, where I figured they'd be serving breakfast by now. On my way, I stopped at an ATM and withdrew $200. The machine dispensed it in $20 bills. It annoyed me that, for all the time I spent in this country, I still had extreme difficulty telling the denominations of the banknotes apart. In America, no one gives a shit about your accent. It's when you squint at their currency that they make you for a tourist. Breakfast cost $15. I paid with a twenty and was handed five singles in change. I left two as a tip. I had a quick shower in my room, read a while and watched a little breakfast TV. Then I headed back down to the beach.

It was after 9 a.m. now and the lifeguards had arrived to take up duty. There were red flags flying from every lifeguard tower. Sunbathers had arrived in force, but the water was closed to swimmers. I approached the nearest tower and asked the tanned lifeguard what the problem was. 'A shark,' he said, matter-of-factly. 'There's a great big shark out there.'

Later that afternoon, the *Miami Herald* posted aerial footage of a large shark marauding close to the shore of a deserted Miami Beach. The footage had been filmed, presumably, around the same time I'd been in the water. The forty or fifty minutes I'd spent swimming that morning – more or less the only time during my visit to this state in which I hadn't been terrified and in fear for my life – had actually been spent treading water in very close proximity to an enormous man-eating shark.

I returned to my hotel room, packed my rucksack and returned downstairs to the lobby. I handed the valet the ticket for my car. I plucked the three one-dollar bills I still had left from my breakfast change out of my wallet. Valet parking had cost me $29, so I figured $3 was about the right tip. I held those three notes in the palm of my hand so I could slip them into his, the way they do in movies. But the valet informed me that my car was being held off site, so it would be at least fifteen minutes before he could retrieve it for me. I put the notes back in my wallet and took a seat in the lobby.

Key West wasn't going to happen. I wanted out of Florida ASAP. When the valet returned I scooped the three crisp banknotes out of my wallet and pressed them into his hand. He thanked me profusely. Then I got into the car and drove due north on I-95. It was a couple of hundred miles before I had to stop for gas. I reached into my wallet for money to pay, and the first three banknotes that came out were three single dollar bills. I'd tipped the valet $60.

I got back into the car and drove with even greater urgency for the Georgia line.

Appraisals

SUSANNAH DICKEY

'This beach is a fungible entity,' I say, the first morning in Brighton. My feet slide and go askew on the stones. A storm is rumoured, but it stays dry. I say I love the wind and he's surprised, but he seems to enjoy how much delight I take in the stiff breeze. In an antiques shop I look at a glass cabinet full of poorly made ceramic animals. I like inaccurate representations of things – the uncanny presence of a lopsided white dog with a red smile; a misshapen bear with bulging eyes. He tries on a hat with a feather and when I say it suits him I mean it. We find a pub with a garden, drink beers with chubby orange wedges in the sunshine.

In the morning I wake up in his bed, sweaty and fully clothed. My skin feels cumbersome; my mouth tastes chemical. I cast my mind back over the night before and realize I can't remember returning to his flat – the last visual I have is of sitting opposite him in a noisy bar. I remember thinking that he looked beautiful. We talked about a young journalist who was recently murdered. He said he thought it was a gloomy portent for what might be coming. I said I thought that seemed less important than the death itself, which struck me as acutely unjust and horrifying. I am not someone who normally responds in an emotional way to news stories, and I said I was surprised this one had had such an impact. There were two shot glasses of tequila in front of us, I recall, though I don't remember us drinking them, and now, lying in my clothes in his bed, I start imagining the most embarrassing scenarios: me, crying in the street having revealed a past trauma; me, putting my hand on his crotch in public; me, hunkered down in a side street, pissing on the ground while he stands watch; me, being pulled away from an argument with a stranger, my eyes wild, teeth bared. I feel myself becoming more and more anxious. I sit up and press my back to the cold wall and watch him sleep, keen for him to wake up so I might infer from his body language what happened.

When he finally does wake, half an hour later, he does not seem upset. I apologize for my embarrassing behaviour and he says that these things happen. I apologize again and he asks how would I react if our positions were reversed. I am grateful for his kindness, grateful that he still wants to touch me, that we can still laugh and be intimate. He reaches out an arm and I lie down and roll towards him. We have frenetic sex – he pulls my hair and squeezes my throat. I don't have an orgasm, but I feel an almost equivalent relief and pleasure when he does.

As we stand in the kitchen, waiting for a taxi to take me to the station, he kisses me and talks about the inevitability of our seeing each other again. I apologize once more for my behaviour. In the taxi the driver, a young man, asks if I visit here often, and I say no, but that I hope I will be back soon. The sky is ripe, and I feel something akin to confidence about my future with this man. It occurs to me that I haven't experienced anything like this before – that my prior sexual relationships have always felt so precarious, so easily derailed by any small indiscretion.

At the airport, waiting for my flight to Ireland, I hear a young child say to his mother, 'They'll be showing the football in Nando's, so we should eat there.' In Boots there is a throng of people in front of the fridge, quivering against each other like atoms. I snake one arm through and lift a bean-and-cheese wrap and a bottle of low-calorie lemonade. On the flight, just before takeoff, I drop the cap of the bottle and it disappears somewhere below my seat. The bottle is mostly full, and I am forced to drink its contents all in one go. Before turning my phone to flight mode I burp into my hand and send four messages to a close friend, the first of which is, 'I am so hungover and this might be the hangover talking but I think I love him and it's a terrible inconvenience.'

*

In the days after my visit I begin to feel a familiar cold dread, the anxiety of suspecting someone has lost interest in you. There is a noticeable change in how he interacts with me, now – his messages are shorter, less zealous, less frequent. We stop entertaining long-winded, elaborate hypotheticals, a dynamic I had enjoyed, as it seemed to rescue me from trying to make the mundane details of my daily life interesting. I liked that our conversations required some imaginative rigour, and I always came away from them feeling edified and giddy. Now, I am invariably the one to instigate contact, and I often have to send him multiple messages over several hours to elicit a response. He is a habitual early riser, and prior to my visit I would often wake to a message from him. That I had at no point taken this practice for granted makes it seem all the crueller that it has now been taken away.

I message my close friend again. I tell her my concerns and say that I need somebody to tell me what I am doing that is so off-putting, to explain how I can come away from an encounter with feelings apparently so different from his. I ask her what it means that I can so consistently get things wrong, when all around me people, her included, seem to walk so effortlessly into happy relationships. She tells me that people are complicated and strange, that the failure of a relationship is rarely a matter of direct causation.

A few weeks later he is in Derry, visiting family. I ask him if we can go for drinks, and we meet in the bar/bistro of a mid-priced hotel. It's a place that has always struck me as particularly atmospheric. I said this to a friend once and he replied, 'Does that just mean dark?' and although that's part of it – they keep the lighting planetarium-low – it's not just that. There's an acoustic intimacy to the dark wood, and hanging baskets drape fronds over the bar, making it feel like you're standing below the abdomen of some great, hairy animal.

From the moment he arrives he seems unsettled. He repeatedly puts his thumb and forefinger to his beard – it has silver threads through it – and jerks it from side to side. He is wearing a dark green turtleneck and tight jeans and desert boots. I have not taken off my coat, because I'm worried the elastic on the cap sleeves of my top makes my arms look fleshy and undulating.

The waiter approaches and asks if he would like a drink. He says no. The waiter leaves and I ask if he is sure he wouldn't like a drink. He says he is feeling a bit low and that drinking exacerbates it. He has only mentioned his depression in passing before, and never in a way that I felt invited further enquiry. I regret not asking him about it when things were better between us. I had wanted to keep things light, but it occurs to me now that I might have seemed callous or uninterested. I suggest a soft drink. He says no.

I sip my gin and tonic while he sits with empty hands and nothing in front of him. He says he can't stay long and I thank him for making the time. I say I know this visit is primarily to see family and I appreciate that he could spare an evening to see me. I ask if he is okay and he says yes, and then I ask if he is sure and he says yes again. The tension makes me drunk-dial confessional. I tell him that I think I am ruining things, that something seems to have changed between us and I am sad about it. I say I don't want things to change, that I think we have a good time together and make each other laugh. I tell him that this is a feeling I often find myself having in relationships – an anxiety that things might be grinding to a slow and irreversible conclusion – and that what usually follows is my pleading and undignified attempt to rectify the situation.

I order another gin and tonic and tell him that if he is feeling hesitant and doesn't want anything more to happen between us then I'd like him to tell me now, that it would be better for both of us if things were concluded in an efficient way. I tell him that I hate a slow waning. He says I am being ridiculous, that nothing is wrong, that he is just very busy with work. I ask him if he is sure and he says yes, and I don't press the matter because it occurs to me that this line of interrogation could potentially alienate him further. I make a few jokes reminiscent of our old style, pretending to be the wealthy and ennui-ridden wife of a financier, drinking rosé at 11 a.m. He laughs, and participates a little, pretending to be the young, strapping gardener with the phallic pruning shears. This gives me hope. I contemplate a third gin and tonic aloud but he says he needs to leave soon, so we go to a quiet corner of the hotel, a brightly lit first-floor corridor. We kiss against a wall. When he puts his hand to the crotch of my jeans and rubs he encounters the thick padding of sanitary towel. I say I am sorry and he asks if I can feel anything through the layers of denim and cotton and absorbent fibres. I say yes. I put my hand between his legs and stroke, the way I might touch a tarantula or a hot plate. A couple emerges from the room next to where we are standing and we leap apart. The couple eyes us, amused. When they have vanished into the stairwell he says he has to go. He books a taxi and we walk to the entrance.

We wait for the taxi in silence, and I try to ignore my palpable desire for him to put his arm around me. When the car arrives he kisses me on the cheek and says that we will speak soon.

A fortnight later, I am back in the bar/bistro, alone. The man at the next table is wearing indigo-coloured bootcut jeans and black dress shoes. His voice is unharnessed.

'And I guess, of course,' he says to the woman sitting opposite, 'the concern with these sorts of arrangements is there will be some fundamental way in which you are incompatible – it doesn't have to be something big, it can be something small, but it niggles at you, you know? But I think it's clear that we don't have that. You know, we go to bed at the same time, we like the same food, we even drink the same amount – last night you had two cocktails after dinner and that was it. Not that you couldn't have had a third, but you know – it meant that neither of us was more drunk than the other. Also, if one person is a much heavier drinker it can cause logistical problems.

For example, I sometimes like to have a beer in the afternoon, but it doesn't preclude me going for a walk in the evening, so it's nice that we're on the same page with that.'

The waitress arrives and hovers at my elbow.

'Would you like anything to drink?'

'Yes, please.' I point at a white wine on the list, scared of mispronouncing the name. 'This one, please.'

'That one is lovely.'

'Oh, good.'

'Glass or bottle?'

'Glass.'

'Large or small?'

'Large.'

The man at the next table reaches forward and takes a chip from the plate next to his pint glass. Beside the chips sits a toasted sandwich, uneaten.

'Another thing that I think has been good is how compatible we are with our day-to-day schedules. For example, neither of us was having to wait for the other to wake up in the morning – we both woke at roughly the same time. That can be a problem, if one person is keen to get up and go and the other just wants more time in bed. That's just one part of it, though. Our timings were roughly equal across lots of things. I think it could be frustrating if two people devote very different amounts of time to different activities – getting ready for dinner, taking a shower, eating. It might seem like a small thing, but these are the portions that make up a day, and if two people are to spend their days together, a drastic difference in how we cut those portions can become a source of contention, over time. I had a girlfriend who spent almost an hour in the shower each evening. She had incredibly long hair that she washed every day. I would have to pace about the house, waiting for her. Of course, it only truly became a problem on holiday, when your itinerary is more closely dictated by your companion. I would have to sit in the hotel room, reading the paper or flicking through the foreign-language channels on the television.'

The waitress brings me my glass of wine. My mouth is so dry I take three gulps as a reflex, and when I set the glass down it is suddenly and conspicuously half empty. The waitress says, 'Another?' and I jump – I hadn't realized she would stay and bear witness. I nod.

'Are you ready to order some food?'

'Yes please.'

'What can I get you?'

'The salad, please.'

'The goat's cheese and beetroot?'

'Yes.'

'That's actually our only salad, currently.'

'Yes.'

'I'm not sure why I felt the need to specify.'

'I'm looking forward to it.'

'It's very good.'

'Good.'

'Is that everything for now?'

'Yes, thank you.'

The dressing that comes in a small silver pot next to my salad is dark green and speckled. I dip one fork prong into the dressing and set it on my tongue. It is sweet, and sticky, and I pour it over the leaves. I spear a cube of beetroot and spread it about in the softening cheese. I kebab a piece of red onion and a few bits of rocket. I put it all in my mouth and think, God, that's so bloody fresh.

The man at the next table now has an empty plate in front of him. I'm not sure when he found the time to eat the sandwich.

'I also think it's good to spend this much time with someone early on, you know? It encourages you to really focus on the other person. Yes, it might seem a little intensive, but I think it's immature to think that a relationship can be compartmentalized or maintained in a vacuum. It's important that it can thrive among the monotony and commonplace events of the day, not just in a two-hour dinner date or cinema visit. Of course, it's a little different being on holiday, but it still gives you a good idea of whether two people can form a partnership even when they might be tired or grumpy or feeling solitary.'

The waitress appears again and I jump a little in my seat. I wonder why I sat facing the wall, making myself so vulnerable to approaching orbiters.

'And here's your wine.'

'Thank you.'

'I thought I would wait until you'd finished your first glass before bringing it, so it didn't get cold.'

'Yes, thank you.'

'Oh, wait – I mean, get warm.'

'Yes, that's great, thank you.'

'I hope you didn't think I'd forgotten about it.'

'No, I didn't.'

'Are you all finished there?'

'Yes, thank you.'

'How was everything?'

'Very good, very fresh.'

'Oh – fresh, that sounds good.'

'It really was very fresh.'

'Would you like to order anything else now?'

'No, thanks.'

'Well just give me a wave if you want anything.'

At 9 p.m. the lighting in the bar/bistro is dimmed further. I lift the menu and hold it close to the candle and read through the options. I do not normally order dessert and I would quite like something else savoury – this was a preference the man and I shared. However, the salad is listed under Main

Courses, and so it seems that to order a starter or an additional main or a side dish now would seem strange, or would be met with scorn.

The man at the next table has brought out his wallet.

'It's quite expensive in here, isn't it? When I booked the hotel I was pleased to see there was a reduction for this time of year. I am not tight with money in the slightest, but I don't like to spend money on things I don't feel to be worth it. We've had a good time, but I think the hotel's peak seasonal rates are a little extravagant for what it is. It's good that we earn roughly the same – it can be an issue if one person is on a much higher salary, especially if the other person is reluctant to have large amounts spent on them. We don't have to deal with that, and when we were choosing activities and restaurants it was good that we were both working from a similar budget. That said, I would never begrudge spending money on a person I was in a relationship with.'

He sets his wallet on the table and finishes his pint. His wallet is brown leather, possibly faux.

I once attended a work conference in Canterbury. The hotel I was put up in was theatrically furnished in a medieval sort of way. The bed was a four-poster and there were sumptuous drapings of fabric everywhere. On arriving in my room after check-in I noticed there were three small, individually wrapped soaps in my ensuite. This seemed excessive, so I opened one and set the other two on the shelf below the sink, thinking that if they were kept unopened and dry the housekeeping staff could put them in another bath-room. However, the following day I returned to my room after a day of meetings and found that not only were the two small soaps still on the shelf, but that I had also been provided with an additional two new soaps by the sink. I washed my hands vigorously, reducing the soap I had opened the day before to a sliver, then unwrapped a new one. I stacked the three, spare, wrapped soaps on the corner of the countertop. On the third day, the stack had been removed and no new soaps had been left. On the fourth, the three wrapped soaps had been returned, so I packed two in my suitcase, thinking I could use them at home. On my fifth and final day in the hotel, not only had the one unwrapped soap been removed, but the housekeeping staff had also disposed of the half-used soap sitting by the tap. It was then I had to open one of the soaps I had packed in my suitcase, and even though I had not gone to the conference with any expectation of leaving with soap, having to give up one of the soaps I had squirreled away the day before somehow seemed like a great injustice.

I realize that I would like to share this anecdote with the man who once sat opposite me. He often complained my stories were too long, with no pay-off. He would say it fondly, teasingly, and it was another aspect of our dynamic that I came to appreciate.

The man at the table next to me stands up, and for the first time I turn in my seat to look at the woman who was sitting opposite him. She has frizzy hair the colour of fallen sycamore seeds, and is wearing pale jeans and a white jumper. I wonder what her voice sounds like. I look back to the man, who is manoeuvring his arms into the sleeves of a black jacket.

'Something I'll have to show you sometime is the album of photos of me when I was at university. I had the most outrageous haircut and dressed quite eccentrically. You showed me some of yours and I remember loving the one of you in the pink dress with the wide, puffy skirt. I like that we both grew up in the same era – I know some men my age might try for a relation-ship with a woman in her twenties, but for me you need that basis of reference, you know? So much of conversation grows from shared experi-ences or at least a shared awareness of certain cultural or social moments, and if you have someone shaking their head and not knowing about the things to which you're referring I imagine it gets incredibly tiresome. Right, shall we go?'

He sets a few notes on the white dish and closes his fingers around an unwrapped mint. They walk out.

I put my glass to my mouth and tip, and it occurs to me that it really is very nice wine, given its very reasonable price. I try to prime myself to expect the arrival of the waitress, but her voice at my right shoulder still makes my diaphragm jerk a little.

'Mind if I take that?'

'Of course not.'

'How was everything?'

'Very good.'

She laughs. 'Fresh?'

I laugh too. 'Yes – fresh.'

'Were you listening to the conversation at the next table?'

'No – not really.'

'It was so strange. I can't be sure, but I think they may have not known each other at all. I think they came on a trip away together as a first date.'

'How strange.'

'I know. He seemed to be giving her a whole appraisal – it was a bit much.'

'Gosh.'

'I can't imagine she'll be too keen to see him again.'

'You don't think so?'

'I don't think he'll ever hear from her again.'

'Oh, I don't know.'

'No?'

'People are complicated and strange, and there is rarely a direct causation.'

She pauses, and looks at me. 'Yes, I suppose you're right.' Another pause. 'Would you like anything else?'

'Just the bill, please.'

'Absolutely.'

Meteorites

TIM MACGABHANN

When Teresa arrives with her autopsy report, Alejandro is standing in the far corner of his office, peering at the map on his corkboard. On the desk behind him, a printer chugs out his report on the morning's shooting. Nothing remarkable had happened. After arresting the cashier at the scene, he shooed the uniformed cop away from the till, collected CCTV footage that backed up the cashier's confession, and went back to the precinct.

'No surprises in this,' Teresa says, dropping the autopsy report onto his desk, beside an untouched slice of chocolate cake.

'Thank you,' Alejandro says, without looking away from the map's rash of little coloured stickers: red for murder, grey for rape, black for common assault. He presses a red sticker onto a point on the map representing the corner of Calle Motolínia and Avenida Independencia where a homeless, unnamed kid aged about twenty-two tried to rob the cashier of a convenience store, only to get shot in the face with a .45 that the cashier claims to have found in a bin in Roma Sur. Although it wasn't nice, it wasn't Juárez, either.

'Whose birthday is it?' Teresa takes the chair in front of Alejandro's desk.

'Sorry?'

She points. 'The cake.'

'Oh. Right.' Alejandro draws a plus sign across the sticker to indicate the kid's death. An 'X' is when the person who dies isn't the assailant. 'I don't know, to be honest. You can finish it, if you like.'

'Nah, I'm sweet enough.'

'Fair point.' Alejandro unlids his pen, writes the day's date on the pink circle. When he sees the digits, a cold weight like a billiard ball rolls down his gullet.

'Have you time for a doughnut this weekend?' Teresa says. They meet up fairly often, more since his wife moved out. Teresa and her wife, Sandra, even cook for him sometimes.

'Ah, I'll have to let you know.' Alejandro crosses the room, lets himself sink back into the chair, and picks up the autopsy report. The striplights hum. The yellow lino seems to pulse. 'I've a thing.'

'Mysterious,' she says, turning the seat of the wheeled chair she's sitting on back and forth on one toe.

Alejandro staples the report together at the corners, then reopens a couple of tabs on his computer. He knows that the inspector's clerk won't read it, still less the inspector, that the pages will remain uncreased as they yellow and fade in a drawer, looked at, perhaps, only when the newish mayor asks them to add up the per-quarter statistics on this or that category of crime, long after the kid has been separated into practice-parts for UNAM medical students; but the knowledge doesn't sadden him, because, although the facts and parts rest nowhere important, they aren't entirely lost, either, except into processes which, while not perfect, or even all that happy, are at least civic or functional in their intention.

Teresa's phone tings: 'Ah, shit. The brother.'

'He OK?' Teresa's brother has had his struggles in the past. Some of them were the same shape as his own.

'Yeah, all good. Exhibition tonight. I'd forgotten.'

On Alejandro's computer screen is a BBC Mundo story about meteorites, showing drone pictures of miles of grass and forest gouged silver with melted slag and ore. His blood is steam, looking at the images, and he has to close his eyes, take a deep breath, hold it, and release before clicking 'print'.

After a time he opens his eyes. For a couple of blinks, the striplights take on a foggy halo, and the dots on his map haze together, before resolving back into a rash on Mexico City's big stomach shape.

'And you?' Teresea says, handing Alejandro the plate.

'And me?' He frowns. 'Me what?'

'Your plans,' says Teresa. 'For the week off.'

'Ah.' Alejandro scratches at his beard. 'That Chinese satellite's due to hit tomorrow.' For weeks he has been trying to imagine the moment. 'I'm taking the bike.'

His head is a blur of everything he has to do to get himself to Coatzacoalcos — lift the tarp, wax the bike, fill the tank, fill the jerrican, fold the tarp, swim, eat, wash, leave — he's in such a burn to be down there on the sand, watching the sea plume, and boil, and whiten.

'That poor satellite.' Teresa gets to her feet, stretching. 'Landing there.' She leans across the desk to press her cheek against Alejandro's. 'Well, be safe, anyway.'

'Same to you,' he says, in a bid not to appear strange.

She frowns a little, then says, 'But, well, I don't know. If a satellite hit Coatzacoalcos, right? I'm not sure anyone could tell.'

'Fair point,' Alejandro says, as he checks the BBC printout against the screen, making sure he has every paragraph.

Most weekends, the roof terrace of Alejandro's building is unbearable: barbecues, Bose Bluetooth speakers, clusters of families trying to outdo each other's braying magnanimity. Tonight, though, the pool and the terrace are all his, because the neighbourhood empties out into Huatulco or Tulum or California once Semana Santa comes.

Jogging out the door and into the rain, his feet slap the concrete, then launch him into a jump that carries him halfway across the pool. The water he displaces slaps the far wall, and then the cool of it belts him full in the chest. He ploughs into his thirty lengths, rain drumming his head when he comes up for breath, rain thundering when he dives again, a rumble of water on water that kills the din of the boulevard fifteen floors below.

His lengths done, Alejandro leans against the wall, the roar of the blood in his head lost in the storm's bigger roar. He sucks in deep lungfuls of that smell of rain on hot concrete, watches the colour drain from the air, rain coursing down his face, water seeming to wash into the gaps between his vertebrae, rinsing out a tiredness as thick as oil. The pipes and gutters mutter and gargle. For a moment it's all so lulling that he begins to drowse, his back softening, his ass sliding from the step, but he catches himself on the balls of his hands and hoists himself from the water.

Inside, two floors down, he takes a shower, dries off, then puts some enchiladas to reheat in a pan on the stove. While he waits for his timer to beep, he sits at the kitchen island to read his printout. One of the photos shows a pit as perfectly round and brown as the birthmark on his heel.

This apartment was once the showroom for the whole building. He made an arrangement with the letting agent, and it saved him the bother of sourcing a bed, a couch, an oven, and so on. No other cop he knows could afford all of this, but no other cop he knows was pensioned off by the Marines, either. He loves the wipe-clean shine of his beige sofas, the kitchen island identical to the one in the hoarding outside, the framed photos of canyons and sunsets which he's stared at so often that they've begun to insert themselves as backgrounds for his own memories. Those photos could be from anywhere, and so could the view through his floor-to-ceiling window – palm trees tossing their heads in the drench, a smog-enhanced patch of evening light, the glint of malls, towers, car bonnets.

Only one photo had to be taken down and stowed behind the couch. It looked too much like the place where he and his division had found those missing cadets that time – desert road, blinding sky, the sand pocked with ocotillo and saguaro, the fence posts parched and split. From the helicopter, it looked like the cadets' arms and legs were trying to spell out letters. Up close, the bodies no longer smelled: vultures and coyotes had worked them over, left only scraps of muscle and fat with the puffy, wavy look of chicharrón pork scratchings, lips scorched to thin black seams like melted rubber.

Bagging up the bodies, Alejandro watched the vultures circle overhead, a big, slow rhyme with the turning rotors.

He eats while reading the article: stuff about last year's meteoroid, the one that pancaked in the air above Ecatepec, showered blistering dust over rooftops and car bonnets, hurting nobody, as lucky a miss, the article says, as when the Tunguska fireball — a two-hundred-foot lump of rock clad in ice — burst half a dozen miles above the earth, flattening hundreds of kilometres of Siberian taiga to matchsticks, instead of exploding a few hours later, above St Petersburg, where it might have destroyed the whole city. For now, though, says the article, the only known fatality caused by an object fallen from space is a dog killed in Egypt in 1911, although a Ugandan boy was injured in 1992 when a tennis-ball-sized bit of pumice struck him on the shoulder. 'All I heard was a whistle, like a kettle boiling,' the boy is quoted as saying, 'and then a thud that knocked me right over.'

Alejandro gets a shiver, thinking what might have happened if that rock had struck the kid's head, and he thinks of Juárez, of that time called 'the war' in all the newspapers, which was fair, given the numbers of dead, and the kind of weapons you'd find lying around, though there were many empty days of barracks-sweat and heat-headaches when the worst fighting was over people's phone-charger cables getting tangled at the sockets. On those no-event days, cabin fever could be fatal, leave you fleeing the place in a bad and careless mood, and there you'd be, en route to the 7-Eleven in an unmarked car, checking Facebook, the window down, and then *bang*, you go spilling down the door of your car, get hauled from the door, dumped to the ground, leaking into the dirt.

Alejandro's fork hovers in the air. His throat tightens. For a moment, he pictures himself from outside the window of his apartment — a lone, heavy-set man at a pristine kitchen island, an image that gives nothing away, like the hoardings outside, or the cover of a book – and then he's able to keep eating again.

In the garage, loading his saddlebags, Alejandro remembers the NA meeting he's chairing tomorrow night, and a spike of panic goes through his navel, and he has to stand there with his hands clasped over his mouth and nose, listening to his breath until the pain goes. Since his relapse he's not been the most active member of the fellowship, just going to meetings, keeping an eye out for the jittering leg, the nibbled lips, the fake agreement-nods that accompany fake listening, before hooking those nervous types for a coffee or some tacos, so they can vent at him instead of relapsing like he did. He's sponsored only one person in the nine months since, a girl preparing to move to Chihuahua with her boyfriend. He texts another regular, his foot tapping out an anxious Morse code on the concrete, until her reply – 'No problem! I'll cover for you! Safe trip!' – pushes a relieved breath out of him, so long and so loud that he thinks of a deflating bouncy castle.

Because it's best not to travel to Veracruz by night, Alejandro sets his alarm for twenty past four and goes to get a blanket for the couch, planning to hit the city exits just as it's brightening.

Half dozing, half watching the late film, he finishes the BBC Mundo article, which closes on a long paragraph about how two chunks of space-trash striking Mexico so close together is an unusual coincidence, given that the last major strike was three million years before, when the Chicxulub impactor struck the region now known as Yucatán and killed all the dinosaurs; but at the same time, the article continues, citing an astronomer from UNAM, the earth is hit by a hundred and forty thousand tonnes of rock from space every single year, meaning that it's best to picture Earth as an apple on a string, turning and turning, waiting for tiny jaws from space to snap at it. Alejandro has to read the quotation once or twice to be sure that this is what the astronomer is saying, but the letters don't shift, so maybe it's just a strange analogy, although maybe, too, it's a because of his sleepiness, which is already tangling threads of the film – about a young black boxer calmly dodging the provocations of his white teachers and the racism of the local police, on his way to some kind of state final — and wrapping them around a dreamed film, in which the young boxer is also a revolutionary, living in a fort of cardboard boxes beneath a highway overpass, somewhere outside a hypermodern but also post-apocalyptic Paris suburb, as he waits for some kind of signal from what's left of his cadre. Alejandro is so gripped that he hates the alarm for snapping him awake, and it takes a second for the urgency to spark off in him again.

He washes his teeth, rinses the grit of sleep-dust from the corners of his eyes, takes the lift down to the garage. Then it's just him on the boulevard, him and a young guy staggering back from some club or party, his shirt open, his shoelaces undone, his steps leaden with drink. For a second Alejandro thinks about offering the kid a lift, but he feels his shoulders tense at the thought of losing time on the road, so he hits the indicator, climbs the rise to the Periférico's second tier, watches the kid's reflection peel from the edge of his rear-view mirror.

Yesterday's smog is still thick and the towers' lights are all still on. Their shapes in the murk could be the enhanced photos of bacteria slides in Teresa's autopsy report the day before. From up here, he can see the mountains, layer after layer in the distance, like torn-out pages. Pictures start to bloom in his head — the satellite's point as bright as a needle, the debris scoring a pink line across the sky – and then he sinks back into the smooth drone of tyres on tarmac all the way to a row of red-brick faux-Alpine restaurants across the state line with Estado de México. As he eases into the hard shoulder, a bunch of men and women leg it from the doorways, trying to wave him over, gabbling prices, menu options, adjectives, but he just breezes past them, pulls up outside the only restaurant where nobody came out to bother him.

Inside, the only other customer is a white man in his late twenties or early thirties, tapping concernedly at his phone while a plate of chilaquiles verdes congeals at his elbow. The radio plays boleros. Alejandro takes a table with a view of the door, watches pines sway on the other side of the two-lane highway. The blue-flour quesadillas, when they come, are pleasantly leathery, but Alejandro can't enjoy them, because he keeps feeling the other man's eyes flicking from his phone to the doorway to Alejandro and back, as though on a circuit. Alejandro turns to face the man: 'Can I help you, sir?'

'Oh.' The man flushes, lowers his gaze. 'Sorry. I didn't mean to interrupt.'

His Spanish is clear, unlike an American's, but it's hardly fluid: he can't roll the double 'r's too hard, and his tongue clunks like a slipped gear going over the gap between each syllable. Maybe he's German.

'That's alright,' Alejandro says, beginning to turn away, but then the guy says, 'You don't mind me asking where you're going, do you?'

Alejandro shuts his eyes for a second. 'Coatzacoalcos,' he says.

The man looks disappointed, says, 'Oh, right,' and turns back to his phone. 'Well, thanks anyway.' He swipes shut his phone. 'I'm sure it'll sort itself out.'

Alejandro sucks in a deep breath to cool the anger geysering up from a point behind his navel. It's sudden, but not in a way that surprises him. His second round of food arrives – another quesadilla, two tlacoyos, and a juice – but he doesn't want any of it.

'Why?' he asks the other man, before he can stop himself.

The man sighs and says, 'Look, what happened is my bus pulled in for food here, and I ended up spending too long in the bathroom. And the driver went off without me. With my bags and stuff.'

'Right.' Alejandro gestures to the waitress, getting to his feet, and mouths at her to wrap the remains of his breakfast. His wife's helmet is still inside the storage compartment under the saddle. The inside of his chest feels like a load of cobwebs are stuck to it, but he's had enough Narcotics Anonymous daily readings ping into his inbox to know that the quickest way to cut your way out of someone else's nonsense is to be nicer to them than you want to be. He points to the man's breakfast. He says, 'Do you want this to go?'

The man's mouth opens a little. Behind the counter, the women who run the restaurant are talking about the cold morning as they wrap his food, but their eyes are on the two men.

Alejandro says, 'I have a bike.' He gives the waitress some money as she hands him a styrofoam burger-shell. 'Intercity buses only go via highways. We'll catch it easily.'

The man scrambles for his wallet as though worried that Alejandro's offer might expire, pays, and then they go outside. As Alejandro fetches the helmet, that geysering anger in him keeps right on going, and in his head he has to repeat a description of the man he's helping — *height: one-point-eight metres; weight: fifty-five kilos; hair: brown; eyes: blue; skin: white* — to quell his wish to lash out.

When Alejandro hands over his wife's helmet, the man looks at it like he's never seen one before.

'Here.' Alejandro loosens the ties of its foam backing so that it will fit over the man's head.

'Oh. Yeah. Thanks.'

'Can I see the ticket stub?' Alejandro says, once his own helmet is on. The man gives it to him, he looks at the bus's vehicle number, and then hands it back.

'You don't want to write it down or something?' the man says.

'Well, I won't be able to look at it while I'm driving,' Alejandro says, climbing onto the bike again. The gentleness in his voice, it's the gentleness he puts on at work, under the bare bulb, hunched over that chair with the one leg sawed too short, a gentleness that tickles the suspect's ribs like the tip of a knife.

'Oh. Right.' He leans over to see if there's somewhere for him to grip, and almost tips the bike over sideways.

Alejandro plants one foot to steady the bike, lifts his visor with his thumb and says, 'You can grab my waist. The jacket's thick. I won't notice.'

'Right, sure,' says the man, and does as he's told.

Alejandro starts the engine. He's forgotten to tell the guy to pull down his visor, but reckons he'll figure that one out himself. There are lots of flies.

A few hours later, Alejandro sits in a pleather booth at the restaurant of his hotel. The kitchen staff have reheated his breakfast for him, but his stomach's an angry, acid churn, and he can't eat a single bite.

Finding the man's bus wasn't a problem. Alejandro caught up with them after twenty minutes, on a bridge above a valley where the fog was rising and falling. The driver pulled over as soon as they were across the bridge, making Alejandro suspect he'd realized his mistake miles and miles back.

If anything, Alejandro made even better time because of all the rush. But now a storm has blown in, in spite of the weather app's predictions. He chose this hotel because it was right on the isthmus of rocks where the satellite is expected to land, but it's also at the dead centre of that storm's black zero.

Rain and spray dash the panes, though it's hard to tell which is which. The map tracking the satellite has zoomed in some more, and now the isthmus has gone from a hyphen to an em-dash.

'How long will this last?' Alejandro says to the waiter who comes to refill his coffee.

The waiter looks out through the huge bay window like he's only just realized it's raining, then clicks his tongue and says, 'Oh, a while, I'd say,' before going to stand by the door to the restaurant, his hands crossed above his groin.

Alejandro sits with his elbows propped on the table and his nose and mouth pressed against his clasped hands. On the wall hangs a framed sepia photo showing a young boy in linen trousers, a tilma, and a straw hat, the sea glimmering behind him, an enormous snake lying dead beside him, so big that the boy's head doesn't clear its dead eye, a soaked, dirty collar of feathers covering half of its body.

Teresa WhatsApps, saying that she and Sandra are praying for rain, because the swelter is unbearable, and the pollution so bad that her photo of their window looks like drifts of mustard gas.

'Swap,' Alejandro replies, then snaps a photo of the rain-crawled window he's sitting in front of.

'We'll take fifty gallons,' says Teresa.

For a moment he looks at the photo he's just sent, trying to picture a dish-washer-size lump of metal speeding in flames towards the earth, but can't convince himself that it will be visible, and so starts eating again, trying to flatten the panic in his belly. As he's swallowing the last mouthful, the waiter returns with a second coffee refill.

'Is that photo real?' Alejandro asks.

'Of course,' says the waiter, without looking. 'This town was full of snakes before they built the waterfront. Fat ones, thin ones, hairy ones. Sometimes there'd be a river of snakes flowing through the grass. You'd have to wait for all of them to pass before you could keep walking.' He finishes pouring with a flourish. 'But that one, the one in the photo, that was the biggest one they ever found. That's the hotel owner's grandfather in the picture.' The waiter gets his phone out and shows Alejandro a photo of a metal sign holed with rust. 'That's why it's called "Coatzacoalcos", see?' The sign shows the verse from Isaiah that mentions a 'nest of vipers', but with 'COATZACOALCOS' writ-ten in Gothic blackletter over where that phrase should appear.

'Strange name for a town,' Alejandro says. 'A bit dark.'

'Well, really it's "place where the serpent hides",' the waiter says, pocket-ing his phone, 'and this port's Quetzalcoatl's last known whereabouts. But the Evangelicals don't want much talk about that.'

'I see.' In the photo, the snake's hanging tongue is coated with sand.

'Want anything else?' the waiter says. 'Drink or something?'

'Just a sparkling water,' Alejandro says. 'Thanks.'

'No problem,' the waiter says, sliding away from the booth, and Alejandro swaps to the seat on the other side, his back to the photo, and to the sea.

The storm abates enough for Alejandro to risk a jog down the waterfront. Wind has blown a dead crab right up to the door of the hotel, and he kicks the crab out of his way, hears it smush on the gravel, before running into the salt-flecked roar of it all. His wife cried when she left him. He patted her on the back while she apologized for getting out of there. She'd requested a transfer to the state hospital in Acapulco so she could be near her father, but she also said that even if her father hadn't been ill, and she hadn't gotten the transfer, then she would still probably have left. She had been pretending that she could be a medicine to Alejandro but she couldn't pretend anymore. He was too sickened by the sight of his hand on her back — that squat dun shape, the fingers like claws — to speak. She packed like she'd been planning it. When he told her, 'I followed you here like a dog!', she just frowned at him as if to say 'Choose a better simile', and wheeled her bag through the door.

Before he could text anybody from the programme, before he could stop and breathe and tell himself what he already knew about the decision, he had the bottle of Centenario Reposado — untouched for months in her drinks cabinet — gone down him. That whole night he hammered that crab hand against the wall, woke to cratered plaster, and called his old division chief to tell him the lot. The division sprang for his dry-out at the Hospital Español in Polanco, thirty days, morning and evening meetings, tri-weekly CBT sessions with a therapist called Dr Gama, a calm woman with big glasses and a framed A3 print of the Wheel of Fortune tarot card on the wall above some potted staghorn ferns. He doesn't remember her patience snapping, not once, not even when he did a runner halfway through a session, not even when she and the orderly found him in the toilets holding a tan horn of his own shit bagged in his underwear, not even when her eyes moved to the chew-marks on the turd; no, she just nodded, her mouth a serious crease, like she did whenever he said something that she found insightful.

Police boats cruise back and forth across the bay, their blue lights winking. The fishermen haven't been allowed out, so they've hung a black-and-red sign from the pier calling the state government murderers and thieves. Apart from that, it's just him on the waterfront, him and some cars that scud past, throw up white fantails of spray. The air whips his cheeks. His feet jolt the tarmac. The street lights reflected in that curve of water look like a necklace of amber beads. As he runs from one pool of light to the other, the glow catches the scars nubbling his forearms and the backs of his hands, from cubes of windscreen thrown at him when a rocket struck his car in Juárez. He and his partner were driving in an unmarked car on the edge of town, near their barracks, past dunes and trash and smashed glass, their tyres ruck-eting over potholes, through a poor but house-proud neighbourhood – couches still wrapped in the showroom plastic, fifty-peso souvenirs of Culiacán and Hermosillo and Guadalajara winking with polish – when, in a scatter of frames, the tarmac buckled, the airbag bloomed, then there was the rain-smell of blood on hot tarmac, his partner hugging the stub of his blown-off leg to his chest, bone marrow leaking out as clear as the wax of a five-peso church candle, all of which he and Alejandro laugh about when they catch up, since the wounded guy's payout had allowed him to move with his family to Ensenada, where he coaches an amputee football team. Thinking of his Facebook photos makes Alejandro quicken his pace along the waterfront, like he might outrun his own jealousy, like the thud of his feet might pulverize all the images in his head.

The rain ebbs to a drizzle, a cooling sprink that rinses sweat from his fore-head. On his phone, the satellite tracker website shows a zoomed-in view of the isthmus, each islet a dot in a basalt ellipsis. The clouds are still thick, so he tells himself that it doesn't matter what he will or won't see, trying to wad down the airbag swell of hope below his ribs, but he still finds himself sprinting the whole way back to the hotel.

He is showered and towelled and waiting in his chair by the window of his bedroom when the satellite hits at last. The look and sound are closer to his imaginings than he thought they'd be, the debris livid red like tracer fire, and the patter of falling parts as loud as Independence Day fireworks, so loud that he jumps in his chair, doesn't land where he was sitting, but rather in the back of a truck in the sandy nowhere outside Juárez, the tussocks as stiff and black as nets in the truck headlights, every breath he draws with a cold nick of woodsmoke to it, the truck wobbling down the bare track, bumping his knees against the knees of the men seated either side of him, clacking the belt buckles of their rifle straps against the muzzles, the stocks squeaking grit against the metal floor of the truck, green and red and white arches of lights in the distance, his gut clenched as the truck passes through the blare of cumbia and reggaetón, through half-wasted laughter rippling from windows and back gardens, through commentary on the Canelo fight that burbles from TVs, until they pull in at the shelter for addicts and the crack of a shot craters the nightwatchman's forehead as he jogs out to see what's happening, and then the sound and air suck into the dream and he's there again, hearing the division chief remind them to make it look like narcos did it, so he shoots the watchman another few times, but loosely, no double taps, then prowls with the others from game room to TV room, via the breezeblocks and rusted spigots in the former Pemex canteen out back where the addicts write their testimonies, then out to the dorms, most of the addicts too sleepy with meds or methadone to scream or run all that much, and besides, his earplugs do for the rest, so it's point and pop, as easy as Xbox, each shot as bright as a comet in the dark.

The sea ignites, a flare the same white as the torch on his rifle, backs and necks and navels and throats appearing in the flash, dropping away, his face a sweaty itch like he's still wearing the ski mask he had on that night, and he empties the whole magazine into one kid who's lying in bed, his headphones on, his book spread on his chest like a shot bird, letters as tiny as ants showing through the torn gap in the cover, the missing 'Pe' in *Pedro Páramo* re-inked in shaded-in ballpoint letters on the page beneath, the cover showing skeletons in their Sunday best lowering a coffin into a dry-looking grave. The book hits the floor. A suck and a rattle like a blocked drain rises from the kid's burst throat.

White light ripples mutely across the water. The people in the rooms either side of his own laugh with relief, say 'Wow', 'What the hell', 'Amazing'. One floor below, someone starts clapping, but then a woman says, 'It can't hear you, Pablo', and he stops. There's a boom. Everything is the colour of metal. The ridges of the waves are the valley floor under the returning jeep's headlights. Patches of Alejandro's head sweat and hurt, but there's no ski mask for him to pull off and get rid of the itch. All he can do is clasp his temples, claw his fingers to the sockets of his shut eyes, pray for so much noise and light that his brain is shaken to mince, but the sea turns black again, the boom doesn't echo, and it's just the crash of the water and Alejandro lying on the bed, the heels of his hands pressed so hard to his eyelids that no further pictures can appear.

He leaves so early the next morning that the nightwatchman does the checkout for him. The air above the sea is pink. Boats are already out dredging for satellite parts. The fishermen have taken down the protest tarp, and now they're collecting their nets.

Riding out of Coatzacoalcos, wind buffeting his helmet, his throat, his ribs, salt gathering in the folds of his jacket, his head a pacified zone, it's like his patrol the morning after the killing, except with none of the pre-hangover hover of the drink's last firings in him, no tight head, no grumbles of the liver, no choppy elation.

After stopping for a piss in a clearing off the forested stretch of road halfway to Mexico City, he walks around for a little while, wet grass darkening the cuffs of his jeans, huffing sap-sharp air into his lungs the way when he was a kid he used to think camels would drink and drink until their humps were inflated. On his phone is a message from Sandra, a donut emoji and a question mark. '8pm?' he answers, and she sends back a thumbs-up.

The back wall of the clearing is a cracked sheet of limestone stretching way up into the trees. The stone has a clammy warmth when he lays his palm to it. He runs a thumb over the calcite traces left by ivy roots that sucked away for years, died, fell away, left a record of their own hunger, a thin illegible cursive that spreads a coldness through his chest, as he hears that shot kid's last gargling. His hands on his hips, he stares at the point on his chest where the coldness is spreading from. He's standing with one foot on a shaky rock and the other on the ground, and some tightness to the muscle puts a spot of warmth in his heel, right under his birthmark. His mother told him once that she'd lost a kid before he was born, and that the mark on his heel was a little good-luck press of the thumb from his ghost of a brother. His skin is all pinpricks of sweat under the biker leathers. He doesn't know what his brother would think of what he's done with the life that was meant to do for two of them, and he's about to stoop, lift the cuff of his jeans, and press his own thumb to the spot, when a heron arrows silently past his nose, out of one stand of firs, into another.

The pistol

MAGGIE ARMSTRONG

The Ryanair bus from Beauvais to Port Maillot was quick and peaceful. Next to me was a friend. We had left school some months before and, for reasons unknown to us, flown to Paris; we had discussed no other places that might be suitable. We stood on a Métro, hunched under our backpacks, reading the names of the stations – Boissière, Kléber, Charles de Gaulle Étoile. The hostel was at the end of a narrow street lined with clothes and bag shops, small bars and tabacs, and Chinese delis with displays of spring rolls and chicken balls and skewered prawns, which I hoped that one day we would eat. We dropped our bags in the dorm then sat at the bar. The barmen were busy and in charge, they drew lines into a book with a plan of the rooms, lit cigarettes, bashed coffee grinders; we spent all our time there, we were never able to leave. It wasn't that we liked their company, it was that we didn't know what else to do. We had no sense that we were in any way worth knowing, nor any awareness of how much we loathed our own guts.

We both had about five hundred euros, and a bed was €25 per night, so we tried to stay in other people's rooms. There was a Danish barman who was very serious but helpful: he gave us maps and local information. At 2 a.m., 3 a.m. he would tour the bar cleaning up while I smoked cigarettes that gave me a sore throat. He would count coins and notes, take apart coffee levers, wipe surfaces, and sweep down the whole bar, occasionally looking my way. His gaunt face radiated sorrow and regret as he went about these duties. At 3 a.m. he stood at the door and flicked off the last light, then tossed his head back. I followed him through the courtyard, up the spiral stairs, to the corridor where he unlocked an empty dorm and I lay on the bottom bunk, frozen still, eying him like a patient might eye her anaesthetist.

'Come on, let me at least put some sheets down,' he said.

'No need for sheets,' I said. He put on a sheet anyway, emptied a pillow into a pillowcase. This is it, I thought, when he kneeled onto the mattress. His hands travelled my body, and my hands travelled his, finding nothing. Nothing at all. He lay with me, hugged my arms and covered my head until I couldn't see. The Danish guy in the hostel liked hugging. That's what he's doing now, I imagine, hugging someone he met on the internet, in a huge city somewhere. 'I would like,' he breathed into my hair, 'just to lie here, and feel your warmth.'

When I woke up, I was in the middle of a dream, my palm was pressed to my pubic bone and sweet holy glory was trickling up through me. I felt the day intrude. The Dane was propped on one elbow, watching me. I sat up.

'What were you doing?' he said, with a half-smile.

'What?' I said and rolled over to pummel myself again, exhaling quietly, thinking, I'll go today and never see any of them again.

'Now that I find cute,' he said. He drew back, looking solemnly down at where his pants were growing large.

'I just need to get some water,' I said and ran to the bathroom where I lay face-down on the cold chemical-smelling tiles and got myself off in as many different ways as I could pack into three minutes.

In the dorm the Dane was tidying up, expertly folding the sheets then zipping them into a plastic packet. I sat on the bed and gazed at him. I thought, if we could get it over with now, he might not tell anyone. Part of me wanted to get it over and done with but the other part didn't want to miss breakfast (cocoa with bread and jam, served by tired Afro-French women in a basement refectory). I took the Dane's belt hook, brought him to me; he covered my hands and shook his head. He smiled marvellously, smiled as if I had given him the most wonderful gift, and that was the last time we were alone together.

My friend and I found different places to stay around the city. On the rug of some Irish boys near Père Lachaise, eating our dinners (tabbouleh cartons and crab sticks) from their dirty plates; why we didn't just wash the plates first I can't say, but it had something to do with not wanting to seem like we existed. In a Canadian folk musician's apartment in Stalingrad, where he would have small dinner parties, serving colourful ethnic stews in bowls made of bread, or three perfect pieces of homemade sushi, and where sometimes, on the pretext of going to the bathroom, I'd raid the kitchen cupboards for breadsticks and brioche rolls. When one of us took out a mobile phone, the Canadian musician said, as if at the very end of his patience with us, 'Put away your gadgets and *listen to the song.*' We got a mattress for two nights, on the floor of a friend's sister in the Latin Quarter, and I would awaken inside a dream and quietly release my bliss my morning dew my droplets of spring, hoping to God my friend was still fast asleep but also thinking, again and again, and again, that it would be worth it even if she woke up, she could disown me, it didn't matter, this was the only thing in the world, it was everything. We would take Métros, traipsing the city for a photocopier, or ads on noticeboards, and return to the hostel bar.

It was different barmen every night, men from all over the world. There were Irish barmen and Israeli barmen and one Italian barman, and a barman from Sydney. There was an English barman, a heavy-set 21-year-old businessman of sorts who part-owned a bar in Belleville but had his own private room in the hostel, with cable TV and stairs to the rooftop. My friend and I called him The Misogynist. Girls would go up to his roof with him, and in the mornings he would brief the company on their performance, leaning in to whisper something, slapping the bar and laughing wildly. The men from all over the world would join in – 'see you in ten minutes', they'd say when he came in with a girl; 'Ramadan is it', when he came in alone. The Sydney guy had a bald girlfriend who kept a rat in her pocket and danced in a strip club. What we had done, moving to Paris, was so obvious, such a schoolgirl affectation, that we pretended we weren't really there. If there was some Parisian fantasy about a quaint little café, with tartan tablecloths and accordions, we didn't talk about it; we just knew that we would settle for the very worst.

The apartments were in La Chapelle, St-Germain, Chinatown, Belleville, Stalingrad. An estate agent met us at Trocadéro and led us up an unsteady brown staircase of the kind girls who dream of Paris are destined to tread. The apartment was cramped but perfectly clean, with cream walls, a single red paper flower standing in a vase on a table for two. We were three now: me and my friend, and a guy from Galway my mother told me to look up, who knew the city and had much more money. There was one bedroom, occupied entirely by a bed which floated in the space like a magic carpet. The estate agent, a man with one arm, said he would be our landlord and our friend, and so for €1,400 a month we had a one-bedroom flat with a view of one corner of the Arc de Triomphe, if you leaned out the window. We handed him the cash, he held the envelope between his stump and his chest and counted the notes with his hand: €1,400 rent plus €1,400 deposit.

The neighbourhood was safe, bourgeois, hostile. The streets were clean and deserted, and I liked to walk them in the evenings with my maps. There was an indifferent concierge on the ground floor with a barking dog. A fruiterie where you couldn't touch the fruit. A tabac, where a man with glasses resting on his nose would look up from his paper and nod an approving 'Mademoiselle', then peer back down at *Le Figaro*. Once I found a fromagerie, stood gazing at the tall yellow cheeses, the wheels of Brie de Meaux, the little grey logs, the swirling bowl of crème fraîche. 'Can I help you?' an old lady asked. 'It was just to have a little look,' I said. 'Well, then what was the point in coming in?' she said.

My friend and I got the bedroom, and the Galway guy got the sofa bed, though my friend and the Galway guy used to stay up late watching TV and smoking hash, and sometimes she would fall asleep with him. In the mornings they lay on and mess-fought, kicking the ceiling, upsetting the furniture, and she would squirt him with a small water pistol. After some weeks, my friend didn't come into the bedroom to sleep with me anymore. Her move, I think, was less about my daily masturbations than about the Galway boy's more relaxed personality: he didn't complain all the time and go around sweeping crumbs from under her, didn't count small change, he enjoyed his days off, earned his money, spent it. They were fast friends, always in the living room when I wanted to read my books: Holocaust diaries, self-help, gently religious books of hope, or *The Bell Jar*, which I found glamorous.

Sometimes, I said 'Shhhh.'

'Hey, this isn't a library,' the Galway guy would say and I would stand up, put on my mother's apron, and cook slightly disgusting meals. Baguettes with Leader Price cheese grated on top and then burnt in the oven, or vacuum-packed cooked chicken, or just tabbouleh cartons and crab sticks, and bottles of Leader Price beer. After dinner, I would take off the apron and say, 'I'm not cleaning up again, sorry, you guys better sort this out,' while they licked their joints and laughed and rolled on the sofas and, while I cleaned and swept, my friend would say, 'You missed a spot there, ahahahahahah,' and she would squirt me. They would pour glasses of white Martini, and get stoned and high, and I would leave.

The neighbourhood was quiet, tree-lined, unfriendly. We understood we were lucky to be close to the Arc de Triomphe, and to the ranked charm of the Champs-Élysées. There were brasseries and pizzerias I imagined I would go to, there was a boulangerie where a smocked woman waited testily with a pair of prongs while you chose a pastry, and a homeless waif stood, frightened and insane. I gave her my Sunday croissant once, she asked for a Coke instead, and I walked away like a coward.

Before all this I had been working in a vegetarian restaurant in Dublin, plating up food. It was the only such restaurant in the city, and every day Ireland's original vegetarians would gather, their eyes strip-searching me for their lunch. My station was the bain-marie, and while on quiet days this could mean simply tossing brown rice around, unsticking the cooked lasagne sheets from the silver trays, and holding a sympathetic smile, on busy days it could be distressing, trying to act normal while my boss ordered me about. 'Claire, service over here'; 'Claire, stop *stirring* that.'

'Claire isn't my name,' I said.

'You *know* what I mean,' she said.

On my first day I fed carrots and cabbage into a grater, and after the lunch rush was told to get on my knees and scrub the stainless steel, all the units and shelves that lined the kitchen. When my paycheque came, it said 'training day: unpaid'. Then Monday, Tuesday, Wednesday, Thursday, €5.75 an hour waking up at dawn, the bus ride, doling out breakfasts, then lunches, performing tasks wrong, waiting for afternoons to end. If I breathed in too deep, I felt I must be very unwell; I couldn't handle the late nights before work, and by the afternoon the healthy thrill of the morning would have worn down into a sneaking inner disturbance, perfectly disguised. One day I was standing at the bain-marie, holding my silver spoon, my nice friendly face fixed, when I thought to myself, *You think you're nice, don't you.* Then I thought: *You. That's me. We're the same thing.* Then, I thought: *We're the only thing.* And I froze, *you froze.* An avalanche thudded down through me, you, the world inside. I took my apron off, went to the bathroom and stood in the mirror. I wanted to see if I was still the same person – or rather, to see if I could go back to being the person I was, before I'd thought about the thing. Standing in the mirror, looking at my strange face, through my crazy bulbous eyes, didn't make me feel at all better. It made me feel a lot worse actually. What I had to do was go back to where I'd been standing and recover authority over the thought. Back at the bain-marie, I would be myself again, as I had been. At the bain-marie, a man was standing, the same man I saw every day. He was a craggy vegetarian man with a coloured beanie hat from which sprang bushy grey and black curls. He was a nice man, but that day he appeared evil. I said I felt sick, took off my apron and left, down the street, wheezing quietly, staring at points ahead.

For some weeks I stayed in my dressing gown, watching video tapes with my mother. When I started to panic I walked from room to room, thinking that if I went into another room, everything would have gone away, like emigrating. But everything stayed the same, the bad place came with me. What I could see clearly, in fast motion, was myself – body, face, eyes – walking from room to room, room to room, looking for a cure, until I was on the roof. And that would be the place to exit, straight down through the breeze. I had no particular urge to die. But it was clear it wouldn't be possible to exist any longer, not like this. I'd have to go. I ate neat, child-sized meals, enough to exist on. My mother took me out to buy a raincoat, to play doubles tennis. On the court, amid well-wishing older women, I was temporarily released – but then, collecting the ball, I would remember the thing. Why, I wondered on the court, netting my serve – why has this come with me, and why with me and nobody else? I was clearly unwell, but how unwell was everyone else, to accept this the way it was?

Or we sat outside the coffee shop in the park, looking onto the bottomless fields, and the winter sun glaring in our eyes. 'It's lovely now,' my mother said, loosening her scarf.

I wheezed, pulled more breath into my lungs, telling myself to breathe in, breathe out again – when had I forgotten how? On the way home, my mother said, 'We need to get you milk thistle, it helps with your sleep. I'll find you a therapist. You're still going to Paris aren't you?' 'Oh I'll go,' I said. What else could you do but move forward? Leave the house, go in the car, go on the airplane, go on the roof? Somewhere this was not.

My mother's therapist asked again and again what my ailment was.

'It sounds a bit obvious,' I said. 'It's that I'm alone. Inside. When I think about it I get really scared.' The therapist, a bony, genteel woman, took small sips from her water.

'But I can't stop thinking about it,' I told her. 'And in a way I think I should look deeper in, investigate what's in there.'

'Don't,' she said.

'Why not?' I said. 'What could happen?'

'Well,' she said. 'Look, I am not a doctor. I just wouldn't go there.'

A homeopath gave me the little glass vial of rock rose, and the minuscule balls of sugar with ingredients distilled from my life story, which I wasn't to let anything touch, not cutlery or toothpaste or anything in the world: everything was contaminated. There was an acupuncturist, who sped around me between each perforation, asking 'Do you look in the mirror for long periods', 'Do you smoke pot?', 'Are your periods short, with thick dark clots?', 'How long has it been since you menstruated?'; I left her office with a bag of Chinese herbal pills I was to take as often as I wanted. A reiki healer, with angels and crystals, who whispered in my ear that she would keep me safe in Paris. An immatsu healer, with angels and crystals, who touched parts of my body until I fell deeply asleep on her plinth. Another therapist out in a beautiful house by the sea. The room we sat in was very fine, with thick furniture in deep greens and golds. Her clothes were very beautiful. 'What happened?' she said, and I told her. I didn't mind telling my life story, it was distracting for a minute.

'Can you pinpoint a time when you weren't afraid?' she said.

'Yes, when I didn't think about the thing. Now I can't stop thinking about it,' and she said nothing at all.

There was the book my mother bought me, *When Panic Attacks* in block letters on a red background. There must have been a GP, because there was a packet of little white pills, one to be taken exclusively at the onset of an attack. It would have a sedative affect.

'Like Valium?' I said, perking up.

'Anxicalm are a baby Valium,' someone said, the GP maybe. 'Don't take too many. These are just a crutch.'

It seemed to me like a very tiny crutch, just big enough for a fairy. My friend and I each swallowed one on the plane to see if anything happened. We slept. My friend was athletic and fun-loving, bright-eyed, she didn't like wasting time and I didn't like to waste things. I kept the pills for special occasions.

Mornings, we took copies of our illiterate French CVs onto the Métro and alighted at distant stops. We walked up and down the Boulevard des Capucines, Boulevard Saint-Denis and other loud exhausting boulevards. We put friendly open-minded personal ads in the magazine. If you weren't going to take your clothes off, there were three kinds of work. Waitressing in the petit café of your dreams – this was the top kind, and totally unavailable. Next was bar work. The lowest, and requiring the least skill, was looking after children.

The guy from Galway worked in a pub and slept late on his sofa bed, waking up to roll a fresh joint and eat whatever I presented him with: a buttered baguette, or a peeled egg which he would bite into imperiously, his head poking from his sleeping bag. My friend had a job in another pub, and I would visit her sometimes, watch her tend the bar with a muscular Swiss barmaid, the two of them swooping for glasses and ice shovels, moving around on the balls of their feet to top up mojitos or lay out rows of shots. I only saw my friend in the mornings, when she slept late with her hair on her face, and I fully resented her. She was enjoying herself. She did man's work, strong and able, and in the apartment she and the Galway guy pinned a dartboard to the wall, and she struck bullseye after bullseye, wearing tiny pyjamas. Once, watching her at her work, heaving a new keg across the bar with the Swiss girl, a hail of dread fell through my body, and I didn't know why. I ran home, took an Anxicalm and slept in a ball.

Late one night, alone in the apartment, I phoned a number on a job advert. I probably played with the cord while the phone rang and rang. A cross male voice answered: 'Oui.'

'Salut, Monsieur,' I said. 'Bonsoir. Je vous appelle parce que le advert, dans la magazine?' My French was always halting and full of question marks – I was a shy, sweet girl in French and in no other context. There was silence, heavy breath. Did I have to spell it out?

'Le advert, pour le modèle sans habille – je suis modèle en Irlande,' I lied. 'Qu'est-ce que c'est le salarie?'

He asked me if I realized that it was two in the morning, and hung up.

One day, we got a phone call from the manager of a Tex-Mex grill. Not just one Tex-Mex grill, a whole chain of them! They had jobs for anyone who wanted a job. I set my alarm for seven, changed Métro twice, and found the restaurant at the end of a big deserted street. A woman annihilated me with one look. I had come the wrong day. I went home, slept, returned again the same time on the following day. She handed me my short Tex-Mex apron and pointed to the touch-screen computer, brightly coloured buttons with food pictures and functions to increase the quantity of an order, or to specify whether a steak should be *bien cuit*, *à point*, or *bleu*. A man ran into the kitchen, shouting at the woman. He threw his apron on the floor, where-upon he stamped on it. 'Allez!' she shouted. 'Putain.' I hadn't known people actually said *putain*. 'Allez, connard.' It was exciting. On the floor upstairs, a very nervous waitress told me that the man had been fired that morning, and today we would be short-staffed. I had not slept more than three hours combined in the past two nights, and my head felt detached, like an empty room in a busy household, a room I had locked myself into by mistake. The Tex-Mex started to fill with people, people who sat alone smoking or in big groups, putting their hands up. I ran to them, then to the computer, where I pressed buttons and strange boxes came up; I couldn't work the system; peo-ple were waving, or tapping me, they came from everywhere. The nervous waitress, frowning now, told me to go outside, and hurry up. I ran outside, where a bald piggy man sat smoking. I took away his espresso cup. Anything else? I asked. 'Danser, bière, numero de téléphone?' he hummed. I ran back inside, tables of three, four then eight big men staring up, hands on the table. 'Vite,' the manager shouted. This was noon. Plates piled with rice and meat bones and half-eaten *hamburguesas* all stacked up, the other waitress punched orders and skidded here and there. 'Vite, alors, putain,' said the manager.

I took off my apron and said that I was going. I handed the apron to the manager. Her hands recoiled. 'No, no,' she said, softly, in English. 'Don't go, please, just help me to clear some of these tables, please.' I went downstairs to get my clothes. I put a bottle of something fizzy in my rucksack, looked around. CCTV in operation. As an afterthought I popped in two bottles of Tabasco sauce. Back in the apartment, I woke the Irish guy with the uncontainable good news that I had a bottle of wine, threw my bag to the floor, and watched the bottle fly out and smash. Glass and wine sprayed all through the room, and on his sleeping bag, his clothes and Discman, the carpet.

'What was the occasion?' the Galway guy asked.

Evenings, I went on walks around the neighbourhood to clear my head. I would break into a long and prosperous stride, and then I would freeze because there it was again. It was always waiting in me, I could go there any time. When I went there, I knew that everything was over, the wind had changed. To live, to be one mind, one set of thoughts, was to be buried alive fighting, hopeless. To live, to be one thinker inside a head was to be held in that very small room, with no people, no door, no window, no light, no refreshment, but it was worse than that because you were the room, you were the door, you were the darkness that had fallen forever. I loved thinking about these things in the most horrible way. Against the wall of that lonely silence my soul threw itself, and fell back, exhilarated!

Sometimes, I picked up the landline to phone my dad and said, 'Daddy,' and went very quiet until he said, 'Oh no, oh no don't cry. Have you got your friends there, have you?' And I left the apartment and walked until my legs felt so tired I had to go home, shut the door, take to the bed, lie face up on the pillow, stare at the bad shapes and sleep. In the mornings, on a sweating pillow, I'd grab my body and come, one two four eight twelve fifteen times before starting the day; it was lonely, delicious, a life sentence, a prison of pointless joy.

There were just three or four bars that were suitable for us, smoke-filled bars with scabrous walls, hippie paint, a lean French crowd. Once a man came and talked to me. He was from Strasbourg, he said. He had sparkling eyes and fat, sensuous lips. Faded blue jeans with rips, and a tight maybe floral shirt with buttons open. He had a strong sexual vibe that was both vindicating and disturbing. He told me I seemed like a very good person, and I said thank you.

He asked, 'But are you happy, you look a bit sad to me.'

I said, 'Most of the time.'

'I'm not happy,' he said, 'and I think that you can help me. I'm so unhappy, because of drugs,' he said. 'I do drugs all the time, I do every kind of drug. Even' – he looked up and bawled with a melting face – 'heroin.'

'Oh I'm sorry,' I said. 'It's very bad for you.'

'I know,' he said, 'I feel very bad, all the time, very black, very depressed, can you help me quit? I think you can help me with your sweet smile' – all of this in French, and the fact that I understood every word made me excited even though I knew I was falling through the trapdoor of a prince of darkness. I leaned in close to hear him properly, my feet glued to the floor. I felt a hand grip my arm – the Galway guy – we had to get the last Métro.

On very odd occasions, my friend and I went out to enjoy Gay Paree. We put on patterned dresses and went to Opèra, where an Englishman at a crêpe stand fried us a crêpe with Gruyère for €6.50, €13 in total. We sat on a wall, picking at the crêpe, which tasted like a salty ball of glue, looked at the names of the films outside the movie theatres, then got the last Métro. To Notre-Dame, to hear musicians play old favourites and drink the stewed tea upstairs in Shakespeare & Company, where Russian ladies stood sentry before the yellowed books on the shelves. My friend met a boy from Toulouse who took her to the Jardin du Luxembourg and the Jeu de Paume and the Île St-Louis and made love to her in his studio bedroom, listening to Air. I found out through the Galway guy, who thought it was simply hilarious; my friend and I didn't talk to each other about things that might suggest we were enjoying ourselves. The boy from Toulouse had a friend, a law student with olive skin and strong shoulders; he was polite, solid. One evening we walked back to his studio bedroom near rue Monge, up six flights of stairs. The studio had a shower head, a single hob, a narrow metal bed. He picked up a guitar and strummed a Jimi Hendrix song. When the song ended, neither of us moved for a long time, glancing at each other and at the tiny room. He asked if I would like a petit café. I said, 'At night! No way! I'd wake up with my heart pounding.' At his doorstep he kissed me hard on each cheek, and I caught the last Métro. We met in Bastille, where he smoked a nargila pipe then unexpectedly fainted, and I caught the Métro, back to the bedroom, the bed, the sound of the French actors on the television which were being used to muffle out the sounds of my good friends' lovemaking, back to sleep and back to waking up; back to relentless ecstasy, all my secrets, quiet and inchoate as an oyster in its shell – dozens and dozens of oysters, closed, lonely, exquisite, dying inside.

My mother phoned on a Thursday to tell me my father had booked an Aer Lingus flight. My father showed up late on the Friday and we ate salade niçoise at the bar of his hotel, not talking as much as I'd imagined we would. My father was big and dark, still handsome and robust, and a little afraid of Paris. He didn't understand the Métro system, he got unnecessary taxis or walked great distances and complained. He handed me a package from my mother: a box of iron supplements, *The Power of Now*, a new relaxation tape, and a fruitcake bound in clingfilm. Plus a cheerful letter with a new prescription enclosed.

He said, 'Christ, there's not a pick on you – are you a vegetarian?' He drained his beer, his gold ring flickered on his tanned finger. 'Are you worried,' he said. 'You're not worried.' He ordered brandy for his stomach problem and drank it down. 'Daddy,' I said. A lump was forming in my throat. 'I don't think you understand. I am losing my mind.'

'You might be finding it, don't rule that out. Call it a night?' he said, and he signed the room tab.

We went to Rodin's sculpture garden; my father looked bored and agitated while I copied *The Thinker* in charcoals. He took me to a very French restaurant that served steak tartare and giant sausages with pots of mustard; to a Mexican place where I had my first margarita; we went all the way to the Café Flore so he could drink a brandy that cost €9, sat in the Musée d'Orsay and drank café crème, sat in comfortable silences that made me fret. On the last night, he took me to a terrifying film called *Chicago* and to a brasserie for steak and chips and two bottles of red wine. 'Are you not having those,' he said, and took handfuls of chips from my plate. He took out his wallet and gave me four fifty-euro notes. 'Buy a pair of shoes, and then buy a therapy session,' he said. 'If you don't like the girl, don't stick it. You have to be smarter than them, you might as well talk to your hairdresser. And don't worry, would you.' He paid the bill, glanced at my full wine glass, shook his head and drank it. When we walked onto the Avenue St-Denis, he said, 'The driving here is barbaric,' took my arm in his strong grasp, looked the wrong way, and swept me right in front of an oncoming car. The driver swerved, beeping the horn at us, and two or three cars screeched on their brakes. 'Well, that could have solved a few problems,' my father said.

It had been a surprise when a lady answered my ad in the magazine. The children lived in a sleepy village reached by a long Métro ride and transfer to the TEF. The three angel-faced children shook my hand and presented me with toys; the girls plaited my hair. I liked the job. It pleased me to prepare small meals and keep somewhere clean. The house was newly built and very comfortable, with a lot of new appliances, an American fridge filled with chilled wine and fresh pasta and French cheeses and fish soup in luxury jars; I cooked elaborate pasta dishes and stuffed my rucksack with Tupperwares of these dishes. The parents worked long and apparently draining hours in offices in the city; their faces were thin and we rarely communicated. Within just a few days the children actively despised me, the person who had replaced their parents. Walking home from school, and from judo and swimming and music and basketball, they kicked each other, and spat, and punched, their brawls veered off the pavement, limbs flew at passing cars; my French commands were shrill and powerless. Over homework, the seven-year-old pretended I was not there; told to eat her sandwich, the five-year-old sighed, 'Ah, bof, tu n'as rien compris.' The three-year-old refused to dress, looked at me cock-eyed and tried to bite me; one day, I hit her in the face. She looked stricken. The blow was mild, I think, and it left no mark on her cheek. I looked around the open-plan kitchen and extended living area: no one had seen. She's too small, I thought. It didn't happen.

The children did their own thing, and I often went upstairs and wrote the sort of long descriptive emails that were common at the time. When a supermarket delivery came, the children tipped the bags all over the kitchen, opened the water bottles, poured the water all over the toilet paper so it stuck to the floor and the walls. Then I would run down and clean up furiously, serve their macaroni from a pan I had burnt at the bottom. The five-year-old would load her fork with macaroni, aim carefully and flick it at my head; then bath time, the dusk of all reason, when they would drown plastic ducks and flood the tiles and I would think about it, the thing. The dark would fall behind my eyes, the doors would shut, constricting every breath; as the girls shrieked in the bath I stood in the mirror, saucer-eyed, and squeezed drops of rock rose from a vial onto my tongue.

*

My mother found a Scottish nun on the rue du Bac whom she said wanted to speak to me. I travelled to the convent on my day off. The Sister was a lively, corpulent woman with strong jowls and eyes that watched me carefully. She bought pastries and quiches from the Bon Marché for my visits and sat me down in the kitchenette, introducing me to all the other nuns as her 'Irish friend'. I felt a fool, and I felt taken in, loved.

'Tell me what's been troubling you,' she asked, unwrapping the foods before her.

'I can't stop thinking about something I'm not supposed to think about.'

'Whatever is it you're thinking about?'

'I can't stop thinking about being on my own. On my own in my mind.'

She tilted her head, pressed her lips together, said that we are all alone, but none of us are lonely if we believe. In God. We ate the microwaved quiche Lorraine which was just slightly cold in the centre; we talked about inspirational books (I gave her Etty Hillesum's diary and never got it back); and I wrote her a stanza of New Age poetry on a Post-it.

'Beautiful, beautiful,' she said, 'it's so reassuring. Tell me now, do you ever think of ending everything entirely?' and I told her that I didn't exactly want to do that.

My mother found a qualified Anglophone therapist on an expat website, and I walked out to see this qualified woman. It was on an upper floor of the Champs-Élysées, in a church, or a children's school, or she was a children's therapist, I don't remember. The chairs were child-sized and brightly coloured plastic. The woman had a leathered complexion, eyebrows like circumflexes, green eyes that could be scary if you wanted. Her mouth was clamped shut, her stare moved between puzzlement and disaster.

'If you tell me you have harmed a child or something I cannot keep that confidential, you understand,' she said.

'Oh yes,' I said.

'Do you feel very down?' she asked. She had a jumpy English accent. 'Do you find it hard to leave the bed? Tell me something – can you remember your home phone number, can you? Okay. Who is your best friend?'

'Can you analyze me a little more,' I said, and she said she had to get to know me first. We talked about drugs that I had never touched, we talked about 'men'. Do you climax, in bed with men, she said.

'In bed with men,' I said, laughing. 'I don't know if I do.'

'Do you ever masturbate?'

'No, not really.' The word engulfed me, fouled my mind. 'No,' I continued, and she let out a laugh now. 'Not regularly,' I said then, 'sometimes.'

'Tell me your deepest fear,' she said.

'It's not a fear,' I said, 'it's actually happening. There's only one of me. I'm inside myself.'

She smirked; this kind of breakdown was maybe all too common.

'And now,' I said, 'every time I think about it, I freeze inside.'

She asked me to describe to her what it was. I gathered myself; like someone confessing something terrible, I had to come up with the best version, the most obvious and relatable crime. 'It's the edge,' I said, adding in a whisper, 'of the universe. I feel maybe I should go down into it and understand what it is?'

Her brows arched up like vulturous wings before flight. 'I don't think you should,' she said.

There was just five minutes left but I confessed to all of it, the pills, the hallucinogens, the frizzy, serrated shapes my friends had all become.

'How old are you, eighteen?' she asked.

I said that I was eighteen.

She sighed. 'I don't know if you might have *done* something to your brain. You'd have to wait and see.' She took the first payment and booked me in for six sessions. I bought Doc Martens with my last two fifties and broke them in back up along the Champs-Élysées.

*

One of those days the landlord noticed streaks of what was definitely just mud on the walls. The mud was from my friends' horseplay, but it looked like shit, he said. Or blood. We had been chatting in the doorway about the ironing board he was appropriating for another tenant. He asked about the large beige stain on the carpet and I said I'd spilled a drop of wine. I presented him with our envelope of rent, and he left. That evening he called to say he had found new tenants. In the days that followed, as he insisted on retaining both our month's rent of €1,400 and our deposit of €1,400, to cover painting and redecorating expenses, I raised my voice and excelled in French. He shouted like a man who had concealed murderous hatred and I shouted back, 'Mais Monsieur, c'est pas possible, regard les spidars morte derrière de la machine, c'était dégueulasse, Monsieur.' He mentioned the shit on the walls. 'Merde? Monsieur, connard, je vous déteste, j'espère que vous êtes morte ce soir, que ta femme tu trouve dans un lac de ton sang propre.' A lake of his own blood. This man, with the disability he overcame with every defiant gesture, this man who had once brought us to his house to serve us Leader Price fondue and watch the lights of Paris sparkle from a window bay, was a thief. I said that my father was a lawyer; he said his wife was. 'Aussi, elle est dégueulasse, ta femme,' I said, before I hung up. It was that afternoon, or another, that I left the apartment alone with my backpack, hauling two suitcases. I hadn't seen my friends in days or weeks. I threw the keys up in the sky and watched them prick the pond in Place du Trocadéro, and I walked to the hostel.

The Dane was off, and there was a new international barman.One or two girls sat at the computers, drinking milkshakes through straws. A song from the nineties throbbed negatively from the walls. The barman served me a pint of beer, which I drank in deep cold gulps. I realized I was panting. In my wallet was the packet of Anxicalm. I was on the second beer when I noticed him, hunched over a plate. It was the heavyset English boy with the rooftop apartment. The Misogynist, sitting next to me. I nodded, and he paused at his meal, and nodded too; we felt embarrassed, because we knew each other only in a crowd and now we were sitting like two friends. He was eating from a wide shallow bowl of spare ribs bathed in a bright red sauce. He tore at each rib with his teeth, tipping the shredded bones onto a stained napkin. We exchanged pleasantries.

'You look a bit depressed,' he said.

'We got evicted,' I said with pride, pointing at the luggage, and he nodded, biting through his next rib.

'What did you do to deserve that?' he asked.

The barman pulled coffee levers, a girl in beads and a cheesecloth dress handed the barman an internet coupon, the Misogynist quickly scanned her body. He licked his fingers and thumbs as he ate, and we talked about ordinary things.

The barman slammed two pints in front of us. The boy ate the last spare rib at a leisurely pace, flicked the bone in the bowl and pushed the plate away. Then he said, 'That was absolutely fucking disgusting.'

By now my heart rate had relaxed, a kind of calm had come over me. I felt as though my thoughts, my long days, were dropping to the floor. I wanted to put my head on the bar; I felt lifted up, hollow, like a balloon rising and bobbing through the space. We sat for a long time looking at each other and away again.

'Aren't you drinking your beer?' I said.

'I don't want it,' he said. He was looking at me very curiously, it must have been the way he looked at people. 'You a smoker?' he asked. His eyes were round brown shining buttons, pieces of plastic soul that ended where they began. He lit a cigarette. I finished my beer, and then I reached out and drank his. I could neither believe nor deny what was happening. He checked his texts and tap-danced his fingers on the bar, drew his chair back. My eye fell to the insides of his thighs, his thick shanks straddling the barstool. I wondered if he was nervous or pretending.

'Want to see the rooftop?' he said. I took the cigarette from his hand and filled my lungs with the delicious smoke, poured the rest of the beer down my throat. We went upstairs and he unlocked his private room. It was spacious, with wooden beams on the ceiling, and humid with sprays and sweat. He threw open the windows, swept shirts to the ground, then came to me.

'Do you want to hear something fucking insane?' he said. 'I find you quite attractive.'

'That's insane,' I said.

I started to kiss him and take off his clothes. I threw him to the bed, unbuttoning his shirt, kissing his face and neck and chest, grabbed at his belt; his jeans might have been cast in metal, they were so hard to break through. I just wanted to burn and blow up and get it over with. I kicked my legs as he got the tights off, unlaced the stupid boots. And everything was ready, he had everything prepared, we were going to another place.

But as I lay back, my eye fell on something on his bedside table, next to his alarm clock and his sunglasses. It was my friend's little water gun, the plastic orange pistol. I picked it up, there was water inside. I hadn't seen the little gun in a long time. He was saying 'What's so funny,' and 'What's up with you,' and 'Fuck, look at that I'm spent. What do you want to do?'

It turned out all he could do was take me up onto the rooftop, which afforded an expensive view of Paris growing dark. There we fell to the floor, and we dry humped. The city looked spectacular from up here, badly built, toppling and shattered. The Eiffel Tower, the Sacré-Coeur, all the broken bits of houses. He moved his hand down my body. He knew what he was doing, he had a smooth and boisterous thrust and he clutched me underneath until I gasped and shouted for more, and I wondered if this counted as anything, could I tell anyone, would he tell anyone, I wanted nobody to ever know. I shouted at him, then gave up, disappeared, alone and afraid with my cheek on the tiles and my heart at home with my mother and my father.

The débutante

LUCY SWEENEY BYRNE

A woman moves to the capital to be with her partner. Even before she arrives she is running out of money, but she pretends she has found a job straight away, so that he won't disapprove of her and ultimately leave her. She joins AA just for something to do (get out there, meet people!), and spends most of her days travelling to and from meetings all over the city. She doesn't share (what to say?), although she does drink secretly in the day sometimes, and the women in her family were all alcoholics.

On weekends she listens to jazz and drinks mixed drinks and does cocaine with her partner on a small oval mirror from the hall, always just a little too much (her, not him, of course), and they go out somewhere and pretend to be strangers picking one another up to go home and fuck, although this happens less now than when she first got there. Now when they fuck it is rare and if it happens at all it is usually after dinner or before dinner and he says 'I love you' as he comes on her stomach.

He has a proper job, and now that she's there and he thinks she does too, he wants them to start thinking about buying a place together (everything in the capital is a process with stages, which, she realizes, is just what proper life looks like – pre-consider, discuss, consider, discuss, co-consider, discuss, research, discuss, preliminary steps, discuss, decide, discuss, pre-act, discuss, act, discuss, complete action, discuss, admire, discuss, celebrate, discuss, briefly enjoy, discuss, find fault, discuss, worry, discuss, regret, discuss, fight, discuss, reconcile, discuss, pre-consider new object, discuss …) – and so she plays along, even though she has no job and is getting ever closer to running out of money.

For her lunch she eats tasters in fancy supermarkets near the AA meetings, wandering the aisles and marvelling at the cost of things. People are so wealthy in the capital and they have so much stuff. Her partner is so wealthy, his friends are wealthy, they all work even more than what she thought to be the correct, expected amount – all day five days a week. Instead, they often work all day and all night on all the days of the week, which is exhausting and leaves no time for much else, but does make them quite excruciatingly wealthy. This allows them to buy life-enhancing teabags that cost six pounds per (small) box, one of which she steeps in hot water and drinks greedily every day, often burning her mouth.

He is not a bad person, he is in fact a very good person. He finds something to be thankful for each day, be it a delicious lunch or glimpsing a beautiful sunset through the window of his office, or from a train. At the same time, he reminds himself that he is constantly moving towards a distant future; one that he can visualize clearly, like the endpoint of a very long run. She is envious of this, amazed, and so she must endeavour to be more like him to participate to concede to defer, to *normalize*. There's nothing else for it – she knows where the other leads. She used to be mad. She used to see through inside eyes. Her tongue used to reach all around the world and her skin used to be on fire. She used to balance on brinks. She used to walk home alone at night. She used to fuck actual strangers. Once she was lost and now she is found.

She runs out of money. She loses weight. She is banned from eating tasters in or even stepping through the doors of certain fancy supermarkets. She stops going to AA, partly because she's heard it all before and partly because however hard she tries she can think of nothing at all to say. Eventually, she is hit on by a man with expensive thick-rimmed spectacles standing outside a plush bar in the middle of an afternoon, a Tuesday maybe, and she is hungry, and she is desperate, and she remembers all of a sudden what it was to be mad, to be her unformed here-and-now self, and so she shrugs an inside sigh and yes, she sleeps with him for money.

She eats the ends of things. She begins fading around the edges. The skin around her fingernails is red-raw and swollen. She's still there, her partner is searching houses within their budget online, he is so happy to be taking this next step with her, he brings her flowers and after he has left for work she eats the heads of them. She is there, she is just managing, then 'poof!' she disappears.

Both too much and too little

IAN SANSOM

Monday 1 January 2019

Woken at midnight by the sound of fireworks and bells ringing. We no longer stay up for New Year. I fall back into restless sleep.

First dream: a great finger hovering in the sky, then a voice crying 'Help, help!' and then a man falling to his death but he doesn't die, he pretends to be a ghost and everyone believes he is a ghost, but he's not a ghost.

Second dream: I'm at home, it's early. I have been for a run. There's a knock at the door. There's a woman standing there, she asks if our eldest son is here. I say he's upstairs asleep, though I know he's not here. She comes in, starts to go upstairs and disappears.

I ask my wife what she thinks the dreams mean. She says they mean that next year we should stay up on New Year's Eve and get drunk, like normal people. She says she really doesn't understand why I bother to write down my dreams. I say, That's what I do: what I do is write down my dreams.

'Seriously?' she says.

Wednesday 3 January

Younger son flies to Paris. I drop him off at the airport, 6 a.m. He has found himself a job, will be staying in a hostel.

'It's definitely all kosher?' I say.

'It's fine.'

'Well, son,' I say, determined not to cry. 'Look after yourself.' Because – what else can you say? I give him a hug, and a hundred euros in a brown envelope. He is much taller than me. That's what I think in the car on the way home: I have a son who is much taller than me.

Sunday 6 January

Go for dinner with my brother-in-law, who has taken early retirement, and his wife, who has left her job and is looking at new opportunities. Mid-fifties. They've just been to Vietnam. They have more foreign holidays planned. These are not wealthy people. They are working-class people. But they have been very careful with money. They have made provision. G*d, I wish I had been more careful with money. All those books. All that coffee.

Watch *SAS: Who Dares Wins*, in which contestants volunteer to undergo a form of Special Forces training. I love it, our daughter loves it. My wife refuses to watch it. She thinks it glorifies violence and is a disgusting celebration of machismo. This year, there are women in the show for the first time. A typical exchange:

'Are you having a fucking baby?' an instructor yells at a woman who is struggling with some horrible physical task.

'No.'

'Well, shut the fuck up then.'

My wife may have a point.

Son rings from Paris. He is living in a room with three other blokes: head-to-toe sleeping arrangements. His roommates stay up all night smoking shisha and talking in Arabic. They all carry knives.

'I won't lie,' he says. 'It's not what I thought it would be.'

'Better or worse?'

'Just …'

'Well, how is he?' asks my wife.

'Fine,' I say.

Tuesday 8 January

My father-in-law rings me in work: would I be able to take my mother-in-law to the hospital? She has a pain in her chest and the GP has suggested an immediate X-ray. I cancel my meetings, get the train home from Belfast, pick up the in-laws in the car, drive them back to Belfast. We're seen relatively quickly, no major cause for concern, and we're back in time for a late dinner: by chance I had this morning prepared some gnocchi with butternut squash, mushroom, sage and pesto, ready for roasting. My in-laws wisely decline, it's late and they have a couple of chops at home in the fridge. All is well.

Something like this every couple of weeks now: my parents, my wife's parents. I wonder how long it can go on for.

'The longer the better,' says my wife.

Tuesday 14 January

For Christmas I bought myself a propelling pencil – a Koh-I-Noor Versatile 5000. It's fantastic: firm but good to hold and crisper than any pencil I have ever used.

On Botanic Avenue, coming home, someone spits on me as I'm walking past. I don't realize for a moment, think about getting into an argument, then change my mind. Fortunately, I have a pack of tissues in my pocket – and the propelling pencil.

Friday 18 January

Now that the boys have left home there's no demand for bacon anymore – daughter is not a big bacon eater – so I've been doing a sort of makeshift Veganuary. Crispy roasted brussels sprouts, and black bean and quinoa burgers, that sort of thing.

We have friends round for dinner.

'D'you know, thinking about it, you do look like a vegan,' says an old friend when I serve my celebrated kale and borlotti minestrone with ditalini, chilli oil and pine nuts. His tone is difficult to interpret.

I first became a vegetarian when I was about 13 or 14, largely to annoy my parents. It worked. The height of vegetarian culinary sophistication back then was a nut roast, but I mostly survived on something called Sosmix, which I bought with my own pocket money from a health-food shop and which was a powdery mix of wheat flour and potato starch that you had to mix with cold water in order to form a sort of mush that you then shaped into sausages as a vegetarian alternative to bangers and mash.

We discuss why more people are turning to veganism at this point in history. The illusion of control?

Sunday 20 January

To give me a break from cooking vegan meals, my wife buys a jackfruit burger from the supermarket. We all agree it is absolutely disgusting.

Monday 4 February

Bought a book of Tom Waits interviews from the War on Want secondhand bookshop, which is no longer the War on Want bookshop – it's Self Help Africa. Tom Waits says of the Keith Richards guitar sound that it has about it something of 'the hair in the gate'. That's exactly the sound I'm going for.

Younger son, on the Metro, on his way to work first thing in the morning – three men rush at him and steal his headphones, try to get his wallet.

Tuesday 5 February

Elder son, living in London, has become the target of a coordinated Twitter campaign. Some stupid thing.

'It's just stupid people,' I say. 'Ignore it. Social media is just stupid people saying stupid shit.'

'It's not, though,' says son.

But it is – it's all just stupid people saying stupid shit. I explain to him the idea of the Two Minutes Hate, from *Nineteen Eighty-Four*.

Visiting London on the train, my dad has had his coat stolen, or has lost it – difficult to know which. Either way, it's gone. Keys, wallet. He's in his mid-eighties. I suggest it may be time to cease his trips to London if I'm not there to help him out.

Obituary in the *Times* of Roy Dean, who was able to do the *Times* crossword in under five minutes. Mr Dean was a diplomat, author and composer – but his crossword skills were by far his most remarkable achievement.

Tuesday 12 February

Cup of coffee with a man who knew Beckett in the 1970s. Seems incredible, but of course not that long ago. My grandfather used to sing the song 'Lloyd George knew my father, my father knew Lloyd George.' It's all just yesterday.

Friday 15 February

I have started counting off the remainder of my days according to an online calculator. Estimates vary. According to one calculator I will die on Friday 22 January 2049; so, I have 10,934 days left. Seems both too much and too little.

Saturday 16 February

The community centre opposite now in a total state of disrepair – graffiti, broken windows. Send email to local councillor.

Drive daughter up to Belfast. The routine seems to be that they have a pre- at someone's house, where they drink vodka, whatever, then go clubbing and drink water.

'Is it fun?' I ask.

'It's OK,' says my daughter.

Unseasonably mild. Our neighbour Clive the Viking sits out smoking till late on the steps of the community centre. I pull up in the car, we get talking. Clive works in learning support at the local tech and is very creative, much more creative than me: painting, writing, making stuff. He tells me about some script ideas he has: they are really great ideas.

'Don't steal those,' he says, stubbing out his cigarette. 'I know you writer types.'

Monday 18 February

Didn't have time to make a packed lunch, but there's a poached egg left over from yesterday that I didn't eat, so I take it to work in a small Tupperware container. A cold poached egg eaten with one's fingers from a small Tupperware container: one of the more miserable lunches I have ever had.

My wife had her purse stolen at the airport. Joint account. Everything cancelled.

Tuesday 19 February

Seven Labour MPs resigned over anti-semitism in the party. Chuka Umunna, Luciana Berger, Chris Leslie, Angela Smith, Mike Gapes, Gavin Shuker and Ann Coffey.

I have absolutely nothing to say about anti-semitism in the British Labour Party.

'You do realize you've started referring to the "British" Labour Party?' says my wife. I hadn't realized.

Yesterday I received a letter from the Department of Justice and Equality acknowledging my application for naturalization as an Irish citizen.

Friday 1 March

Eason's on the way home – completely empty. The Eason's guy says there are rumours that it's closing. In the past year or so the two big banks in town have closed, most of the cashpoints have gone, the shopping centre is now boarded up.

'TK Maxx and Boots are going as well,' says the Eason's guy. 'And then that'll be that.'

Fed up with Veganuary, which we just sort of kept going. We have a Chinese takeaway. We have a Chinese takeaway maybe once or twice a year. Delicious.

'We should do this more often,' I say.

'If we did it more often it wouldn't taste as good,' says my wife.

Tuesday 5 March

Fly to London to deliver corrected manuscript of new book to HarperCollins: urgent, overdue. When I arrive, my editor is too busy to see me. Am redirected by staff at front desk to take the manuscript to the loading bay at the back of the building.

Wednesday 13 March

Teaching a class at the Irish Writers Centre. On the Belfast train on the way back, there is no one in my carriage at all – not a soul. Half-lit, beautiful journey home. Like travelling inside a dream.

Thursday 14 March

My old colleague and friend the poet Ciaran Carson rang to let me know he has lung cancer and is dying. The doctors say he has six months, max. I tell him I love him, and thank him for all he has done for me and for others. Thanks to Ciaran, it was a surprisingly matter-of-fact conversation.

Saturday 16 March

51 people killed and another 49 injured in attack on a mosque, Christchurch, New Zealand. Jacinda Ardern, the NZ prime minister, very impressive.

Wednesday 20 March

Theresa May has asked the EU to delay Brexit beyond 29 March. My wife says I have started referring to 'the Brits'.

'You do know you are an actual Brit?' she says.

I ask Kaz the barber how he is. He says that this is one of those times he feels he can't speak good enough English to express himself properly. He says it breaks his heart. My heart is broken, he says. I assume he means

Brexit. It turns out he means a friend of his, another Turkish barber, who was killed in a car crash on the Crumlin Road last week.

Monday 25 March

Met a colleague for a cup of coffee. The man at the table next to us seemed to be listening in to the conversation: as we were leaving, he leaned over and said, 'I couldn't help overhearing your conversation' and engaged us in a long conversation about our conversation.

Wednesday 27 March

Younger son texts a photo: he is grinning, with his new girlfriend, who is Spanish. They look so young and happy. They are outside Pitzman's, the Jewish falafel place we used to visit in Paris when he was a child.

Thursday 28 March

Received an email from a man who lives in the flat in London where we lived twenty years ago. He continues to receive post for us and would like to forward it to us. First: I'm amazed that he's still receiving post for us twenty years later. Second: I'm amazed he's bothered to seek me out in order to send it on.

But third – after twenty years?! How much post has he amassed in that time? I offer to pay for postage. Am expecting a crate of mail.

Everyone is watching *Fleabag*. Everyone is talking about *Fleabag*. Why is everyone watching *Fleabag*? I don't know.

I watch *Fleabag*. Zingers, bantz, high-jinks glances straight-to-camera. I can see the appeal. It's funny. Also, strikes me as a very English form of grief work.

Monday 2 April

Meet a man, a visitor to Belfast, who is well travelled, highly intelligent. I ask him what he thinks of Belfast.

'Ian,' he says – he is American, so he uses my first name a lot – 'Ian, let me tell you something. I have travelled to a lot of places. I have seen a lot of things. And I can tell you that this little old city of yours is a very special place.'

'It's certainly that,' I say, in my usual jocular fashion.

'You know,' he says, deadly serious. 'It really reminds me of somewhere back home.'

'Really?' I say, laughing. 'Where? Hoboken?'

'Manhattan,' he says.

I have no reply to this.

'Manhattan,' he says again. 'Belfast is like Manhattan in miniature.'

The food, he says: Mike's Fancy Cheese on Little Donegall Street. ('They do this awesome raw-milk cheese. And the sourdough bread is to die for.') I have never been to Mike's Fancy Cheese. 'And all your little boutique bakeries, and the restaurants! You're spoiled for choice.'

'Have you tried the Gregg's on Botanic?' I say.

He agrees to show me round some of Belfast's culinary hotspots. 'And is it true that in the University Library here you have the door to Narnia?' he asks.

'I don't think it's the actual door,' I say.

Monday 4 April

Fly back from England, straight into work. Visiting my parents most week-ends now. Expensive, but cheaper than a care home. They are clinging on. They refuse to talk about death, decline, arrangements, anything. They just want things to remain the same.

On my phone, pointlessly looking up synonyms for decline (decadence, declension, declination, decline, degeneracy, degeneration, degradation, descent, deterioration, devolution, downfall, downgrade, ebb, eclipse, fall) I come across deringolade, which means 'a rapid decline or deterioration (as in strength, position, or condition)'. G*d forbid deringolade.

Saturday 13 April

Fly to London to see Peter Blegvad playing in Clapham – used to work with him, years ago. Meet elder son and his girlfriend. We haven't met before. They are thinking of moving in together. She is Latvian. Very nice young woman. Plain-speaking. Very witty. Perfect English. (First language Latvian, second language Russian, then German, French, some Ukrainian and Belarusian, English.)

'She has perfect English,' I say to son, when we are alone for a moment.

'You can't say that,' says son.

'Why?'

'It sounds racist.'

Girlfriend returns.

'So, what do you think of your son having an immigrant girlfriend from a former Soviet socialist republic?' she asks.

'Great,' I say.

'That's the right answer,' she says.

I seem to have passed the test.

Monday 15 April

Younger son gets hold of my wife on the phone, panicked. He's just leaving work, there are people running through the streets, shouting, some sort of glowing fog or mist in the sky. What should he do? My wife says run. Then the networks go down.

Tuesday 16 April

Younger son sends photos of Notre-Dame in flames. He started running, but then found that others were going towards the burning building. Eventually there were huge crowds. He sends a video of people singing 'Ave Maria'.

Wednesday 22 April

Listening to *The World Tonight* on BBC Radio 4. Ukrainian comedian Volodymyr Zelensky has won a landslide victory in the country's presidential election. More than 73 per cent. A comedian. It's either clowns or comedians.

Thursday 23 April

In Botanic Gardens, by the University Library – lunchtime, it's sunny, I am talking to my friend Will on the phone when three men sit down next to me on the bench. Sports-casual wear, tattoos. They turn up their music, I get up to move away, they follow me, and start shouting 'Fuck off home, you fucking Muslim.'

I walk towards the library.

'What the hell was that?' says Will, who's still on the phone.

'That's Belfast,' I say. 'People get confused about the beard and stuff.'

Thursday 2 May

At work, between meetings, I turn on BBC Radio 3 – catch the beginning of Schubert's Fantasia in F Minor. Over the years I must have listened to it a hundred times. I burst into tears. I don't know what that's about. Recesses of feeling.

Saturday 4 May

We travel to England for a friend's birthday – classic depressed Northern town. Incredible number of beggars. Almost all of the shops either To Let or boarded up. Feels … Brexity. Feels like home.

At the birthday party I meet a woman who introduces herself as 'The Porn Lady' – she advises pupils at school about sex. 'Dick pics, that sort of thing,' she says. I also meet a businessman who has retired early to organize a church soup kitchen, which has seen a massive increase in demand since the introduction of universal credit: he is furious with the Tory government, absolutely disgusted. I then talk to a woman who is dying from a rare form of leukaemia and, finally, a Christian missionary from Pakistan, who left the country when the school where he taught was attacked by the Taliban, killing staff and pupils.

Staying at our friend's house: her budgie says, perfectly clearly, 'Bugger', repeatedly, and 'Sod off.'

Thursday 16 May

One of my oldest friends – M – rang about a month ago and asked if I would like to accompany him on a trip to Poland. I've known M for about thirty years: we met as students. M is now a wealthy tech investor. Our lives could not be more different. His father died a couple of years ago and he's been wanting to reconnect with that side of his family, hence the trip. Would I accompany him, he asks, because – well, because.

Being a wealthy tech investor, M has money and 'people', so he arranges the flights and the hotel. I have neither money nor people and have certainly never flown business class, which turns out to be similar to economy, except for a nice chicken salad, a small glass of wine, and a bit more leg room.

We're picked up by a driver. M does not use his name when being picked up at airports – it is inadvisable, apparently, for high-net-worth individuals to have drivers pick them up with their names written on a little board, for fear of being kidnapped. I had no idea that M lived in fear of being kidnapped. He tells me about some of his security measures at home.

Our driver tells us he lived in Dublin during the early 2000s, not far from where I used to stay when I was working in Dublin, on the north side.

'It was not good,' he says. 'It was worse than Poland.'

He worked many jobs in Ireland, but in the end he wanted to be in his own country.

'You should live where you belong,' he says.

'I don't know where I belong,' I say, joking, but not joking.

'You should find out,' he says.

He recommends that while we are in Poland we try the pierogi, the Tyskie beer, and the vodka.

'And pork,' he says. 'You must eat a lot of pork.'

I say I will do my best.

It's late by the time we arrive, so we decide to just drop off our bags and go for a quick drink. In the main square we're stopped half a dozen times by young men in leather coats asking if we would like to visit a 'titty bar' or meet some pretty girls. We do not want to visit a titty bar or meet some pretty girls. 'Gay bar?' suggests one of the leather-jacketed men. The bar we end up in doesn't serve Tyskie – only Heineken. And neither of us is in the mood for pierogi, or for pork.

Friday 17 May

Our driver meets us at 7.30 a.m.: we have to leave Kraków early to avoid the rush hour. On the way, M fills me in on some of his family history. I know bits and pieces, but he's been doing some research. Estonian Jews, most of them ended in the Riga ghetto. Through Yad Vashem he's been able to get in touch with some long-lost relatives: he now has an invite to a Haredi wedding in Israel. M quizzes me on what I've read: I've read the Martin Gilbert book, of course, and Paul Celan, Primo Levi, Elie Wiesel, Bruno Bettelheim, Hannah Arendt, Imre Kertesz, Aharon Appelfeld, Tadeusz Borowski; the kind of things you might expect a literary type to have read. M recommends the Robert-Jan Van Pelt book, *The Case for Auschwitz*, Raul Hilberg's *The Destruction of the European Jews*, the Laurence Rees books, David Cesarani, Saul Friedlander, and Nikolaus Wachsmann's *KL: A History of the Nazi Concentration Camps*. He says he'll send them to me.

We pass a McCafé and a KFC Drive-Thru and then there's an enormous car park – dozens and dozens of coaches – and a complex system of entry, and you get equipped with a set of headphones and a tiny receiver, and before you know it you're in, wandering around. There are thousands of people; a feeling of barely contained chaos. At various points, you're asked not to film or take selfies, but people continue to film and take selfies.

At lunchtime, I buy a cheese and tomato sandwich from a snack bar in the car park. M eats and drinks nothing all day, despite my coaxing. There's nowhere to sit, so we squat down on the floor. After lunch, it's a five-minute drive to the ruins of the gas chambers, which are fenced off by white plastic chain-link fencing.

As we're leaving, right outside the main gate, a man drives past with a monkey puzzle tree sticking out of the boot of his car. When M's driver arrives to pick us up the radio is playing – unbelievably – Chris Rea's 'Road to Hell'.

On our return to the city, M says he needs to make a few business calls. We arrange to meet later for dinner. The restaurant we are eating in offers a 5-, a 7- and a 12-course tasting menu. I can't even imagine a 12-course menu so we compromise with the 7-, which is all amuse-bouches and palate-cleansers, and froths and foams. M asks the sommelier to match some wines. 'And we'll have a bottle of your finest Champagne,' he says.

We make a toast.

Well,' he says, 'what the fuck else are we supposed to do? Cry?'

Saturday 18 May

On the Saturday, M decides he wants to spend some time alone back at the camp: he's brought a stone from home that he wants to place somewhere. I spend the afternoon wandering around the city. Near the National Museum I find myself caught up in a big Pride march. Everyone is very friendly. I'm given a small rainbow flag to wave. It's not until we reach the main square that I realize that the big noisy crowd up ahead is not in fact another part of the Pride march coming to join us but a far-right counter-demonstration. Things get quite lively quite quickly. There are a lot of riot police wearing white helmets, all incredibly tall. I slip away into the crowd and pocket the rainbow flag.

Sunday 19 May

I suggest that we visit the old Jewish quarter. M can't get a signal on his phone, so we soon get lost. Everyone we ask for directions says they've never heard of the Jewish quarter. 'Synagoue?' we say. 'Synagoga?' And as a last resort, 'Jews? Żyd?' Everyone ignores us. Eventually we manage to tag on to the end of an Oskar Schindler tour. 'And this,' says the tour guide, 'is the courtyard and the stone steps where Stephen Spielberg filmed an important scene in the film.' On a wall someone has pinned up laminated images from *Schindler's List*.

We wander around a flea market. M has never possessed a menorah. He says he'd like to find a menorah somewhere here – maybe in the flea market, or in a junk shop. It would be like an act of restitution. But there are no menorahs in the junk shops.

In the car to the airport, the driver asks if we have been in Poland on business: M certainly has the look of a man who has been here on business; me, maybe less so. M hasn't spoken to anyone since we arrived about why we're really here – I've been chatting to everyone, solicitous, blasé, oblivious – but we're nearly done now and on our way home, so he explains. The driver then tells us that his family had to leave their home because people returned claiming that it was their home. 'But they didn't need to maintain it or pay taxes on it for all those years,' he says. 'It's not right. And you know what, the Jews weren't exactly saints during the war.' At the airport, as he lifts M's luggage out of the car, the driver says, 'Just remember, there are two sides to every story, my friend.'

Thursday 30 May

Kaz the barber is rather philosophical, and depressed, as usual. He's tired of people, he says. Racists. Christians. All sorts of crazy, he says, tapping a finger to his head. The other barber says he has a headache, because he is fasting – Ramadan. Kaz says he doesn't fast. He says Ramadan is nonsense. 'My life is complicated enough,' he says, 'without all this.' We talk about the boxing instead.

Sunday 2 June

Anthony Joshua vs Andy Ruiz Jr last night. Joshua the undefeated, unified WBA (Super), IBF, WBO and IBO heavyweight champion. He's in incredible shape. Andy Ruiz Jr – well, he's a big fat guy. Ruiz won by a technical knock-out in the seventh round.

I call my dad. We reminisce about Mike Tyson vs Buster Douglas, Lennox Lewis vs a person whose name we can't recall – other big heavyweight boxing upsets.

'That's why people like it. It's unpredictable,' says my dad. The boxing, he means.

Tuesday 4 June

Late last night, driving home from Armagh, having given a talk to some community groups, listening to jazz on Radio 3: Avishai Cohen Trio, Gwilym Simcock, Floating Points. Joyous – art. Then get home and before going to bed, sit down with a cup of tea to read the paper. Article quoting recent migration figures – 3.6 million refugees from Syria now in Turkey, 1.2 million from Venezuela in Colombia. And in other world news: rise of Vox, the populist party in Spain; Salvini in Italy; Bolsonaro in Brazil. Then a long article about the divide between the city and the provincial towns and rural, and another about how the Tories are running down the clock on Brexit, hoping that everyone will just get tired of it and want it all to be over. Restless sleep.

Thursday 6 June

Find what I'm looking for, a clip on YouTube of Tarkovsky talking about *Andrei Rublev*: 'Some sort of pressure must exist; the artist exists because the world is not perfect. Art would be useless if the world were perfect, as man wouldn't look for harmony but would simply live in it. Art is born out of an ill-designed world.'

Father-in-law's eightieth birthday. Everyone has a few drinks. At the end of the evening a friend of the family offers to show us his tattoos. He has a lot of tattoos. He takes his trousers off, revealing tattoos commemorating the exploits of the 36th Ulster Division at the Battle of the Somme, on his inner thighs. I'll be honest – they're not great tattoos.

Wednesday 12 June

It has rained on and off for two weeks, so much that somehow rain has started coming down the kitchen walls.

In England for an external examiners' meeting. At dinner, a woman tells me an incredible story about the thieves who ripped the catalytic converter out of her Toyota Prius, for the platinum, and the time she almost died when a passerby shot an arrow through her living room window using a crossbow. Another man, the son of Holocaust survivors, is a film scholar. We get talking about Alfred Hitchcock's cameo in *North by Northwest*, where he fails to catch a bus. Back in my hotel room I look up Hitchcock's cameos – there's a YouTube supercut. People say – I'm on the internet forums now – it all started because he just needed somebody to fill out some foreground space in a shot, but what began as a momentary necessity became a bit of a lark and then a superstition and an obligation. He got fed up with it in the end. I watch the clips again and again. My favourite – particularly poignant – is the one in *I Confess* (1953), a film I have never seen, where Hitchcock is seen crossing a street at the top of a long staircase. Something about this, the Hitchcock cameo. I can't get at what it is: something to do with loss and memory? It is 3 a.m. by the time I go to sleep.

Friday 27 June

Younger son assaulted on a bus late at night – punched in the head. He's had most of his possessions stolen in the hostel.

'What is going on in Paris?' I say.

'Just don't tell Mum,' he says.

Wednesday 17 July

Obituary in the *Guardian* for Andrea Camilleri: 'Had Andrea Camilleri died in his 50s, his obituary would certainly not have been published in the *Guardian*. His death might have been noted in the cultural sections of the odd Italian newspaper and it would doubtless have merited a substantial article in the journal of Italy's pre-eminent drama school, the Accademia Nazionale d'Arte Drammatica, where Camilleri was for many years in charge of teaching directing.' Most cheering. Still time.

Tuesday 23 July

At my parents', fixing a toilet seat – my father had banged his head trying to do it, and then couldn't get up.

The bolt rusted and stripped. Hottest day of year so far. I have to get a hacksaw to cut through the bolt. Buy and fit new toilet seat.

My mum spends most days in a chair, asleep, then little bursts of energy. So far this summer we have already had one nighttime A & E run, plus usual hospital trips.

Boris Johnson has been elected Tory leader, of course. There had been something in the papers about a big argument with his girlfriend. Commentators said it might have an effect on his chances. But of course it didn't.

Sunday 25 August

Dad thrilled with England dramatically winning third Ashes Test. *Poldark* on TV – my mum's favourite. And *Peaky Blinders* – my dad's. *Peaky Blinders'* success relies partly on the spicy dialogue and high-gloss production values, but what really makes it interesting is that it corresponds to the current national predicament: a programme about people beset by endless and apparently unresolvable problems, which can only temporarily be resolved through brute force and violent argument.

Thursday 29 August

Article in the *Times*: 'Russian border guards have seized 4,100 wild tortoises after they were smuggled out of Kazakhstan in a trailer disguised as a consignment of cabbages.'

Sunday 1 September

My parents both sick all night, after I made scrambled eggs for dinner. My dad buys the eggs from a farm up the road – free range, unmarked eggs, unmarked boxes. Kept on a warm kitchen shelf. Stupid of me. Lucky things weren't worse. By evening they're recovered. My dad gets up to watch *Peaky Blinders*. In this episode a man gets tar poured over him in revenge for his having crucified someone, and in another scene a man appears to be beaten to death in a Quaker meeting hall.

'You can see why your mum doesn't like it,' says my dad.

Wednesday 4 September

The BBC's political editor on the radio this morning said, 'There is only one certainty: nothing is certain.' On the contrary. Everything is certain: election, Brexit, etc. The Supreme Court ruled that the Prime Minister's advice to the Queen to prorogue parliament was 'unlawful, void and of no effect'. It will make no difference.

Monday 9 September

Spent the weekend settling daughter into college in Scotland. She has dyed her hair blonde, has taken all my Murakami novels, and my supply of Moleskine and Muji notebooks.

'Will you be OK?' I say.

'Of course I'll be OK,' says daughter.

I do not doubt her. Tears on parting.

Stayed overnight in Edinburgh with my wife, before she travels down to England for her new job and I fly back to NI.

'That's it then,' I say.

'Well,' says my wife.

The children have gone. We're all living in different countries. The old homestead no longer a home. What's coming next not entirely clear.

Tuesday 10 September

Only me in the house now. I make a stir-fry – far too much food for one person. I have been making stir-fries for years. Without thinking, I absentmindedly put my fingers into the hot oil. If I had a therapist I'd talk about this with my therapist.

Friday 13 September

Younger son returns from Paris, packing up to go to music college. He plays – again and again, incessantly – Coltrane's fourteen-minute version of 'My Favourite Things'.

Sunday 22 September

At breakfast, while examining my dad's hands – completely crippled with arthritis now, huge hands like barnacled old crab shells, gnarled and seized in position – he suddenly starts speaking in German. He loves the German language, always has – prefers it to English. He recalls being in Germany back in the 1950s, on manoeuvres with his SBS unit, supporting the British Army of the Rhine. Amazing stories I've never head before: reconnaissance missions, swimming, diving, laying limpet mines. He rarely if ever talks about this stuff, though I've always known he was in the Royal Marines/SBS. Just something we never talked about.

There's a garden centre up the road does a Sunday lunch with dessert and a cup of tea – 'and a proper nice rich gravy' says my dad – for £7. I say I'll treat them. But when we arrive there are long queues. People start queuing from 11.30, apparently.

Thursday 3 October

Second, third, fourth day of Rosh Hashanah? Can't remember. On the train home a woman got on and sat down next to me. Out of the corner of my eye I noted her hair, which was blonde and luxuriant, and her coat, which was powder blue. And the smell – perfume, hairspray, cigarettes and chewing gum. Overwhelming. Took me instantly back to school. Discos, girlfriends.

Saturday 5 October

Our remote control for the telly is broken: there seems to be no way of fixing it. Something to do with the buttons. I've tried everything. I have simply given up watching TV, but my wife – who is home for the weekend, and who is very resourceful – takes a bread knife and prises off the top. I can now control the television by jabbing at the exposed sensors with a small screwdriver.

Sunday 6 October

Call came from Glenn at work, around 10 a.m. I knew what it would be. Ciaran died last night. Called a couple of people. Made a sort of spinach curry for dinner – not nice.

Thursday 10 October

Notice in the *Irish News* yesterday: Requiem Mass for Ciaran Carson tomorrow at St Therese of Lisieux Church, Somerton Road, Belfast, 10 a.m.

It is twenty years ago now that Ciaran invited me to give a reading in Belfast. I was a stay-at-home dad, had just published my first novel. I have no idea how he came across the book, but he wrote to invite me to come and do a talk. We met in a bar beforehand. I duly arrived, young and earnest, clutching my book, and so the long conversation began. We talked about books – we always talked about books. And we drank – I think – white wine. In later years it was coffee. (He occasionally offered what he called shamrock tea. I stuck to Nambarrie.) It was raining outside – always. I remember Ciaran stood for a while, smoking in the vestibule of the bar, talking about the etymology of the word 'vestibule'.

When I left Northern Ireland to work in England for a few years, Ciaran gave me a gift – an Esterbrook dollar pen, a beautiful mottled grey model from the late 1930s, with a lever-filling mechanism and fine chrome detailing. The pens were manufactured to provide the working man with a quality writing instrument: a democratic pen, Ciaran called it. In recent years, at his many book launches, I would produce the pen and ask him to sign his new book.

'It's your pen, Ciaran,' I would say.

'No,' he'd say. 'It's your pen.'

Irish literature's great and the good at the funeral. They have flown in from all over the world. Paul Muldoon reads a poem, etc. I keep that little Esterbrook dollar pen in my pocket.

Tuesday 22 October

I fly to London for a meeting, having got up at 4.30 a.m. for a 6.30 flight. The person I am meeting – who lives in London – doesn't turn up for the meeting. I am left waiting for three hours. Visit my wife, who is staying with her sister.

Sunday 3 November

There has been rioting in Chile, there are wildfires in California. I'm at my parents'. They go out and get lost in the car – again. Somehow got caught up on the M1, ended up on nine-hour detour. High drama. When they eventually arrive home I make them a cup of tea and they both fall asleep in chairs watching *Strictly: The Results*.

Rifling through an old copy of *Moby-Dick*. Post-it notes, marginalia. Ishmael remarks that 'whenever it is a damp, drizzly November of the soul, when the impulse to knock people's hats off for no reason gets too strong, it is time to take to the sea.'

Tuesday 26 November

The Chief Rabbi Ephraim Mirvis – 'not a patch on the last bloke', according to my dad – says that anti-Semitism is a 'poison, sanctioned from the very top' of the Labour Party.

There is a colleague at work who uses the most incredible range of vocabulary, so incredible I have started noting the words down (so incredible, in fact, I wonder if he's doing it for effect, if he's looking up words in the dictionary every morning). So far, in notebook: lucubration, banausic, enfilade.

Saturday 7 December

Meet old friends for dinner. One of them is refusing to pay TV licence – BBC is a complete rip-off, he says. We get into an argument about Rupert Murdoch and Fox News.

Friday 13 December

Boris Johnson wins landslide victory. Of course he does.

Friday 20 December

I buy a gammon for Christmas – the children are all going to be home for

Christmas. We'll all be together. They all love a gammon at Christmas. Even I eat gammon at Christmas. At the till in the supermarket the woman says, 'See the gammon I have at home? It'd choke a donkey.'

This puts me right off the gammon. I put it in the freezer.

Monday 30 December

Reading the *Guardian*, p. 16: 'Alasdair Gray, giant of Scottish literature and art, dies aged 85'. Why do I love Alasdair Gray? Why did I love Alasdair Gray? I think about it.

Why do I love Alasdair Gray? It's because he is the only writer I can think of who pulls funny faces in photos. Seriously, that's why.

Notes on contributors

MAGGIE ARMSTRONG is working on a novel.

EOIN BUTLER is a freelance journalist based in Dublin.

SUSANNAH DICKEY's first novel, *Tennis Lessons*, will be published this summer.

TIM MACGABHANN is the author of *Call Him Mine*, a novel.

IAN SANSOM's most recent book is *September 1, 1939: A Biography of a Poem*.

LUCY SWEENEY BYRNE is the author of *Paris Syndrome*, a collection of stories.